GEORGE

The Man Who Watched the Trains Go By

Translated by Stuart Gilbert
with revisions by David Watson

PENGUIN BOOKS

PENGUIN BOOKS

Published by the Penguin Group
Penguin Books Ltd, 80 Strand, London WC2R ORL, England
Penguin Group (USA) Inc., 375 Hudson Street, New York, New York 10014, USA
Penguin Group (Canada), 90 Eglinton Avenue East, Suite 700,
Toronto, Ontario, Canada M4P 2Y3 (a division of Pearson Penguin Canada Inc.)
Penguin Ireland, 25 St Stephen's Green, Dublin 2, Ireland
(a division of Penguin Books Ltd)
Penguin Group (Australia), 250 Camberwell Road, Camberwell, Victoria 3124,
Australia (a division of Pearson Australia Group Pty Ltd)
Penguin Books India Pvt Ltd, 11 Community Centre,
Panchsheel Park, New Delhi – 110 017, India
Penguin Group (NZ), cnr Airborne and Rosedale Roads, Albany,
Auckland 1310, New Zealand (a division of Pearson New Zealand Ltd)
Penguin Books (South Africa) (Pty) Ltd, 24 Sturdee Avenue,
Rosebank, Johannesburg 2196, South Africa

Penguin Books Ltd, Registered Offices: 80 Strand, London WC2R ORL, England

www.penguin.com

First published as *L'Homme qui regardait passer les trains* 1938
This translation first published by Routledge as
The Man Who Watched the Trains Go By 1942
Reissued, with minor revisions, in Penguin Classics 2004
Published as a Penguin Red Classic 2006

3

Copyright © 1938 by Georges Simenon Limited
2005 (a Chorion company). All rights reserved.
Translation copyright © 1942 George Routledge & Sons Ltd

ISBN-13: 978-0-141-02587-2
ISBN-10: 0-141-02587-5

I

How Julius de Coster Junior soused himself at the Saint George tavern, and how a bolt from the blue struck his second-in-command

As far as Kees Popinga personally was concerned, it cannot be denied that at eight that evening there was still time; his destiny still hung in the balance. But time for what? Could he indeed have acted otherwise than as he actually did, convinced as he was that his acts that evening had no more significance than those of the thousands of evenings which preceded it?

He would have shrugged his shoulders derisively if anyone had told him that his life was abruptly to take a new turn, and a reproduction of that photograph standing on the sideboard, showing him in the midst of his family, with one hand idly resting on the back of a chair, would figure prominently in newspapers all over Europe.

And if, in introspective mood, he had set himself to discover if there were anything in his make-up that might predispose him to such a tumultuous future, nothing is less likely than that he would have thought of a certain queer, half-guilty feeling that crept over him whenever he saw a train go by – especially a night-train, with all its blinds down, rife with mystery.

Also, if anyone had told him point-blank that at that very moment his employer, Julius de Coster Junior, was seated in the Saint George tavern, deliberately drinking himself fuddled, it would merely have struck him as an attempt to pull his leg – a form of humour for which Kees, who had settled ideas about people and the world at large, had a distinct aversion.

Nevertheless, unlikely though it was, at that moment Julius de Coster *was* in the Saint George tavern drinking gin.

And in one of the suites at the Carlton, in Amsterdam, a certain Pamela was having her bath before starting out to Tuchinski's, the fashionable cabaret.

But how could these facts concern Popinga in the least? Or the fact that in Paris, at Chez Mélie, a small restaurant in the Rue Blanche, a red-haired young woman, Jeanne Rozier by name, was dining with a man called Louis and, as she helped herself to mustard, asking:

'Are you working tonight?'

And the fact that in Juvisy, near the railway marshalling-yards on the Fontainebleau road, a garage-proprietor and his sister Rose were . . .

No, none of this yet existed; it lay in the future – the future of Kees Popinga, who at 8 p.m. on this Wednesday, 22 December, had not the faintest premonition of it, and was just preparing to smoke a cigar.

What he would never have confessed to anyone, for it might have sounded like an indictment on his family life, was that after the evening meal he felt extremely drowsy. It wasn't because of the food, for, as in most Dutch households, the evening meal was little more than a high tea: bread and butter, thin slices of cheese, cold sausage, and the like, with perhaps a sweet as well, and only tea to drink.

More likely the stove was responsible – no ordinary stove, but a majestic contraption of the very best make, in sleek green earthenware with chromium-plated fittings. It did more than heat the living-room; its heat, its breathing, so to speak, seemed to set the rhythm of the life of the household.

The cigar-boxes stood on the marble mantelshelf. Popinga selected a cigar with care, sniffed it, then held it to his ear, squeezing it gently – because there's no better way of judging the condition of the leaf, and, anyhow, no connoisseur omits to do this.

As usual, no sooner was the table cleared than Frida, Popinga's daughter, a brown-haired schoolgirl of fifteen, dumped her exercise-books on it, under the lamp, and gazed at them for some minutes with the far-away look in her dark eyes that was always an enigma to her parents.

And, as usual, Karl, Popinga's boy, who was thirteen, offered his forehead to be kissed, first to his mother, then to his father, and, after kissing his sister, went upstairs to bed.

The stove was roaring away cheerfully and, by force of habit more than anything else, Popinga asked his wife:

'What are you up to, Mum?' He always addressed her as 'Mum' because of the children.

'Oh, I've some more pictures for my album.'

She was a woman of forty with an air of amiable dignity matching that of the house and its appointments. One might have said of her, as of the stove, that she was the 'best make' of Dutch wife; indeed, it was one of her husband's fads to talk about 'the best make' of everything.

The chocolate they ate was an exception, being admittedly second-grade, and they kept to this brand only because each packet contained a picture, and the makers supplied an album which, when the collection was complete, if ever, would contain coloured illustrations of all the flowers in the world.

So Mrs Popinga settled down with the big album in front of her and fell to sorting out her pictures, while Kees twiddled the knobs of the wireless, and presently the only sounds in the room were the trills of a soprano and now and again a tinkle of crockery from the kitchen, where the maid was washing up.

So heavy was the air that, instead of rising, the smoke of his cigar hovered round Popinga's face. Now and again he slashed his hand through it, as in a country lane one brushes away the floating strands of gossamer.

He had been doing these selfsame things night after night

3

for the last fifteen years, till every movement, every attitude, had become almost automatic.

Tonight, however, just before half-past eight, when the soprano had ceased singing and a monotonous voice was reading out the closing prices, Popinga uncrossed his legs and said in a doubtful tone, gazing at his cigar:

'I wonder if I shouldn't go and see if everything's all right on board the *Ocean III*.'

A silence followed, filled by the drone of the stove. It lasted long enough for Mrs Popinga to paste two more pictures in her album and for Frida to start a new page of her exercise-book.

'Yes, I really think I ought to go and see . . .'

At that moment the die was cast. There was just time left for Kees Popinga to smoke another inch of his cigar, to stretch his legs, to listen to the Hilversum orchestra tuning up – and then he entered the web of fate.

From now on, every second had more to it than all the seconds of his past put together, and each of his acts had as much importance as those of any of the public men whose most trivial doings are featured by the Press.

The maid brought his grey winter overcoat, his fur-lined gloves and his hat. She slipped galoshes over his shoes, while he raised obligingly one foot after the other.

He kissed his wife and daughter, noticing once again how impossible it was to guess what the latter was thinking about – assuming (which was far from certain) she was thinking about anything at all. As he entered the hall he wondered if he should take his bicycle, a most beautiful machine, nickel-plated all over, and equipped with gears.

Finally he decided to go on foot. As he stepped on to the pavement he turned and looked back with satisfaction at his house. True, it was not the biggest in the street, but he himself had designed it, and he was convinced that it was the best planned and most pleasing to the eye.

And the street, in fact the whole district – a new one situated just off the Delfzijl road – was to his mind quite the healthiest and most attractive part of Groningen.

Until now Popinga's life had been made up of small satisfactions of that type; the most solid type, when one comes to think of it, for no one can deny that a first-class object is first class, that a well-built house is a well-built house, or that the meat from Oosting's is far and away the best in Groningen.

The air rasped his cheeks, but it was a dry, invigorating cold. His rubber soles crunched frozen snow. As, his hands thrust deep in his overcoat pockets, a cigar in his mouth, Kees strolled towards the docks, he was genuinely anxious about the *Ocean III*.

It was not a pretext he had given himself, though there was no denying it was pleasanter walking in the crisp, frosty air than drowsing in an armchair in his stuffy dining-room. But he could never have brought himself to countenance the thought that any place could be more agreeable than home. Still, countenanced or not, the thought was in his mind and it made him blush when he heard a train go by and caught himself having a peculiar sensation, a vague, nostalgic yearning for – he knew not what!

The business about the *Ocean III* was very real, and Popinga's nocturnal visit of inspection no less than his duty. He was managing clerk to the leading ship's-chandler in Groningen, indeed in all that part of Holland. The firm of Julius de Coster & Son supplied everything that seagoing ships require, from tar and tackle to fuel-oil and coal, not omitting food and drink of all descriptions.

The *Ocean III*, which was due to sail at midnight so as to clear the canal before high tide, had given in a big order late in the afternoon.

Kees could see the ship in the distance, a three-masted clipper. The approaches of the Wilhelmina Canal were deserted;

the only obstacles in his way were hawsers, over which he stepped adroitly. Then, with the ease of a man used to such missions, he climbed the pilot's ladder and walked straight to the skipper's cabin.

Stretching a point, one might say that even now an avenue of escape, the last one, still lay open to him. It was still possible for him to turn back. But how could he know that fate was giving him his last chance? As he opened the cabin door, he was confronted by a burly red-cheeked man who greeted him with a volley of expletives.

For an amazing thing had happened, quite unprecedented in the annals of the House of Julius de Coster. The tanker which was due to deliver the fuel-oil at seven – Kees himself had given the instructions – hadn't turned up. And not only had the tanker failed to materialize, but nobody had been near the ship and none of the ship's stores had been delivered.

Five minutes later, Popinga was hurrying off *Ocean III*, still murmuring excuses to the irate skipper, assuring him that there had been a misunderstanding and he would fix things up at once.

His cigar had gone out. He was sorry now that he hadn't taken his bicycle, and, throwing dignity to the winds, he broke into a run, so horrified was he by the thought that, for lack of oil, *Ocean III* would miss the tide and might even have to cancel her sailing to Riga. Though Kees did not follow a seafaring life, he had been to a naval training-school and had a master's ticket. And he couldn't help blushing for his firm, for himself, for the merchant service – for the whole wretched business!

Sometimes the head of the firm returned to the office after dinner, and Kees had hopes of finding Julius de Coster there. But he drew a blank at the office. Without a moment's hesitation he started off, panting heavily, to his employer's house: a large, stately looking building, but, like most of the dwelling-houses in the centre of the town, older than Popinga's, and not so well appointed. Not till he was on the doorstep, with his finger on the bell-push, did it occur to him to throw away the stump of his dead cigar and start thinking what to say.

There was a sound of footsteps approaching from a considerable distance, a spy-hole opened in the massive door and a maid's eyes peered at him indifferently. No, Mr Julius de Coster wasn't at home. Nothing daunted, Popinga boldly asked to see Mrs de Coster, who was a high society lady, daughter of a Crown Commissioner of one of the Dutch provinces, and the last person one would think of worrying about such matters – except in a grave emergency.

At last the door opened. Popinga had to wait for quite a while beside a tubbed palm at the foot of the marble staircase. Then the maid beckoned, and he was shown into a room bathed in a discreet pink glow, and was confronted by a lady in a silk wrap, smoking a cigarette in a jade holder.

'I can't think why you came here. My husband left some time ago to finish off some urgent work at the office. Why didn't you go there instead?'

Thereafter he was never to forget that flimsy wrap, the mass of lustrous brown hair coiled on the nape of her neck, and the superb aloofness of the woman as he backed out of the room, stammering apologies.

Half an hour later, all hope of getting *Ocean III* off had to be abandoned. Kees had gone back to the office on the off-chance that he had passed his employer on the way to his private residence without noticing him. Then he had started down a brightly lit street in which the shops were still open, in view of the approach of Christmas. A voice hailed him:

'Hello, Popinga! Where are you off to?'

They shook hands. It was Dr Claes, a child specialist, who belonged to the same chess club as Popinga.

'Aren't you coming for the match tonight? I hear our man's quite likely to beat the Pole.'

No, he didn't feel like going. In any case, it was always on a Tuesday he went to the club, and today was Wednesday. He was still feeling the effects of his run through the frozen air; his face was red and his breath hot as fire.

'By the way,' Dr Claes remarked, 'Arthur Merkemans looked me up this evening.'

'Well, I must say he has some nerve . . .'

'Just what I told him!'

And Dr Claes walked away towards the club, leaving Popinga with another load on his mind. What had prompted the doctor to tell him this about his, Popinga's, brother-in-law? After all, isn't there a black sheep in every family?

As a matter of fact, the term 'black sheep' was too strong; there was nothing much against him, really. Merkeman's biggest mistake was to have had eight children; but in those days he had quite a good position at an auctioneer's. Then one day he had lost his job and remained for some months without employment, because he aimed too high. After that he had rushed to the other extreme and taken any job going, and things went from bad to worse.

Now everyone fought shy of him as a professional cadger, always talking about his eight children and bemoaning his hard luck.

A trying sort of relative to have! For quite a while Kees fumed inwardly against this ne'er-do-well brother-in-law of his, whose wife had taken nowadays to doing her shopping without a hat on . . .

Well, there was nothing to be done about it. He entered a tobacconist's and bought a cigar. It struck him that he might as well go home by way of the railway station; it wasn't really any farther that way than along the canal. He knew he wouldn't be able to refrain from saying to his wife:

'Do you know, your brother's been to see Dr Claes!'

She would know what that meant, and sigh; but she wouldn't say anything. That's how she always took it!

He walked by Saint Christopher's Church and then turned off into a narrow street where the houses had massive doors with iron knockers and the snow was banked a foot high on the pavements. He was about to switch his mind over to plans for Christmas, but desisted, knowing too well that after the third streetlamp other thoughts would waylay him.

It would be nothing very serious, no more than a vague unrest, but invariably it came over him when he passed that point on his way home from an evening's chess.

Groningen is a highly moral town in which, unlike such a city as Amsterdam, one runs no risk of being accosted by ladies of the street. Nevertheless, a hundred yards from the station there stands a certain solidly constructed house, highly respectable in aspect, whose door opens to the lightest knock.

Never had Kees set foot inside it. But he had often heard people talking about it at the club. As a matter of fact, he had always managed, in one way or another, to eschew temptations of that order.

All the same, whenever he walked past that house at night he couldn't help imagining things, and on this occasion his glimpse of Mrs de Coster – whom hitherto he had always seen fully dressed – in *déshabillé* had made him more impressionable than usual. He knew that she was only thirty-five, whereas Julius de Coster ('Junior' though he still officially was) was nearing sixty.

He walked past the 'fun house', as it was called, and only halted for a moment to watch two shadows moving behind the blind of one of the first-floor rooms. The station was already within sight; the last train was due out at five past midnight. Before he came to it, on his right, was the Saint George tavern, which held for him, though in a milder way, something of the glamour of the house he had just passed.

In the old stagecoach days a famous hostelry known as the Saint George Inn had flourished here, and a small tavern had sprung up beside it, known then as the Little Saint George. The hostelry had vanished years ago, but the tavern had survived. It was situated in a basement, its windows level with the pavement, and was patronized chiefly by English and German sailors as a last port of call after other pubs had shut.

Somehow Kees could never refrain from glancing through its windows, though actually there was nothing much to see: only grimy oak tables, wooden benches, stools and, at the far end, a bar-counter presided over by a fat man with a goitre so enormous that he was unable to wear a collar.

Why should the Saint George tavern give the impression of being a place of ill fame? Was it because it stayed open till two or three in the morning? Or because there was a bigger array than anywhere else of bottles of gin and whisky on the shelves? Or merely because the tap-room was in a basement?

As usual, Kees glanced through the window. A moment later he was flattening his nose against the pane, to make sure he wasn't mistaken, or, rather, to convince himself he was.

There are two categories of café in Groningen: the *verlof*, or temperance establishment, and the *vergüning*, where alcoholic drinks are served. Kees would have blushed at the mere thought of setting foot within a tavern of the latter class. Indeed, he had given up playing skittles because the skittle alley was in the back premises of a *vergüning*.

And there in the tap-room of the Saint George, a *vergüning* of the deepest dye, sat a man who, to all appearance, was none other than the worthy Julius de Coster Junior! If Kees had rushed away at once to the chess club and told Dr Claes or anyone else that he had just seen de Coster at the Saint George tavern, the news would have been received with sympathetic looks and friendly suggestions he had better go and consult his doctor.

There are some people about whom it is indecorous to joke, and Julius de Coster was one of them. Even his beard, which had no like in Groningen, inspired a certain awe. So did his demeanour and his funereally black garb, not to mention his famous hat – a cross between a top-hat and a bowler.

No, Kees decided, it was unthinkable that Julius de Coster should have shaved off his beard; equally unthinkable that he should be wearing a brown suit, and a badly cut one at that! And as for his being seated in the Saint George tavern, with a big-bellied glass all too obviously filled with gin in front of him – well, that settled it; Kees's eyes had certainly deceived him.

But just then the man turned his head towards the window and he, too, had a look of surprise and craned his neck to get a better view of the face pressed to the pane.

More startling still, he gave a little wave of his arm, that meant:

'Come along in!'

And Kees entered, fascinated as animals are said to be by a snake's stare. He entered, and the proprietor, who was washing glasses, bawled to him from the bar:

'Why don't you shut the door behind you, like other folks?'

Yes, it was Julius de Coster, and no other. He pointed to a stool, saying:

'Been down to *Ocean III*, haven't you?' Then, without waiting for a reply, added a phrase never heard on his lips before: 'And I'll bet they're raising merry hell!'

Again without a pause, he said: 'How the devil did you know I was here? Been spying on me, eh?'

The oddest thing was that he didn't seem in the least vexed, and made the last remark in a friendly tone, with a twinkle in his eye. He signed to the man behind the bar to fill the glasses and, changing his mind at the last moment, decided to keep the bottle on the table.

'Please listen, Mr de Coster. There's something happened that . . .'

'Finish your drink first, Mr Popinga.'

It was his custom to address Kees as 'Mister', as indeed he addressed even the humblest of his employees. But tonight he gave the word a slightly ironic intonation and seemed entertained by his managing clerk's obvious discomfort.

'If I tell you to drink – and my advice, my friendly advice, to you is to finish off that bottle if you can manage it – that's because it may help you to digest what I'm about to tell you. I certainly didn't expect to see you tonight, but I'm glad you're here. You will notice that I, too, have had a few drinks – and that will make our little chat all the more agreeable, I feel sure.'

He was drunk – Popinga would have sworn to it. But drunk as one who's used to being in that state, and takes it lightly.

'It's tough luck on *Ocean III*; she's a fine ship and her charter-party requires her to be at Riga within the week. But what's happening is far tougher luck on some other people, including you, Mister Popinga.'

While speaking, he poured himself out another drink. Kees noticed a big, soft-looking parcel beside him on the bench.

'What makes it even rottener luck is that I don't suppose you've any money put aside, and you'll be without a job, like your brother-in-law.'

Popinga thought: here's someone else talking to me about Merkemans!

'Do finish off your glass . . . You're a level-headed man, Mister Popinga, and I can be quite frank – brutally frank – with you. So let me tell you that tomorrow the firm of Julius de Coster will be in liquidation – and what's more, the police will be on my tracks . . .'

Luckily Kees had drunk two glasses of gin in quick succession. He could tell himself that he wasn't seeing straight, that the man in front of him, stroking his shaved chin complacently, his lips curled in a sardonic, diabolic grin, wasn't really Julius de Coster.

'You won't grasp straight off what I'm going to tell you – that would be expecting too much of a true-born Dutchman like you. But, little by little, it will soak in, Mister Popinga.' Each time he said 'Mister' he used a different tone, as if savouring the word.

'The first thing I've to say will get you on the raw, I fear. I know you have a very high opinion of yourself – and I won't deny you some ability – but it throws a pretty dismal light on your intelligence that, though you were my managing clerk – indeed, my right-hand man – you never spotted what was going on. Listen! For over eight years, Mister Popinga, I've been indulging in speculations that were, to say the least of it, extremely risky.'

It was even hotter than at Popinga's home, and here it was an aggressive heat that an ugly cast-iron stove, of the type used in railway stations, launched at one in sudden waves. There was a reek of gin, sawdust on the floor, and the table was mottled with rings of moisture.

'Have another drink, please, and bear in mind you'll always have *that* consolation anyhow. As a matter of fact, on the last occasion I saw your brother-in-law, I'd an impression he'd lit on that interesting truth . . . So you went on board the *Ocean*, did you?'

'Yes, and I went to your house as well . . .'

'And I suppose you saw my charming wife? Was Dr Claes there by any chance?'

'Really I . . .'

'Now don't get flustered, Mister Popinga! For the last three years almost to the day, for it began on a Christmas Eve, Dr Claes has been sleeping with my wife.'

He went on drinking, taking little puffs at his cigar. As the minutes passed it seemed to Kees that de Coster was getting more and more like those sinister bas-reliefs of Satan which figure on the portals of some Gothic churches, and from which one has to tell the children to look away.

'Perhaps I should add that I had my compensations. Every week I went to Amsterdam to enjoy the company of Pamela. You've heard of Pamela, eh, Mister Popinga?'

So calm was his demeanour that it was hard to imagine he was drunk, whereas Kees, simpleton that he was, blushed at the mere mention of Pamela. For hadn't he too, like many of his fellow-citizens, nursed wild, impossible hopes . . . ?

Just as Groningen has only one 'fun house', so it can boast of only one cabaret where dancing goes on into the small hours. Kees had never set foot in it, but he had heard many stories about Pamela, its leading light, a rather over-ripe, dark beauty, with a captivating lisp. She had spent two years in Groningen, and her exotic costumes had been the talk of the town, though proper-minded ladies looked away when they passed her in the street.

'Well, it's I who've been keeping Pamela and paying for her suite at the Carlton, in Amsterdam – where, by the by, she introduced me to some other charming little ladies, friends of hers. Now are you beginning to understand? You're not too tight, I hope, to follow what I'm saying? Take my advice and don't miss a word – you'll never have such a chance again. Tomorrow, when you think it over, you'll see the world with different eyes, and perhaps it'll be the making of you.'

He gave a short laugh, drank off his glass and filled it again, then filled up that of his companion, whose eyes were growing hazy.

'I know it's rather a lot to take in at one go, but I shan't have an opportunity of giving you a second lesson. So ram as much of it as you can into that bullet head of yours. Think of the damned little nincompoop you used to be! What? You want a proof of that, do you? Well, here's one – and it touches your business capacity, as it so happens. You've got your master's ticket, and you're pretty vain about your nautical knowledge, aren't you? You were the man whose special duty it was to look after the five clippers owned by the House of Julius de Coster. Well, it completely escaped your notice that one of them carried practically nothing but contraband cargo, and that another clipper was sunk, under my orders, for the insurance money.'

Was it an effect of the drinks or due to some other, less obvious, cause? Anyhow, at that moment, a singular change came over Kees – a preternatural calm, leaving him from now on incapable of the least reaction: incapable of doing more, it seemed, than listen to the other's flow of words.

And yet . . . ! The mere names of the five clippers flying the House flag should have been enough to jog his fancy into action: *Eleanore I*, *Eleanore II*, and so on. All five named after the lady Kees had just seen in her dressing-gown, a long cigarette-holder between her lips – Mrs de Coster, in fact, who, according to her husband, was the mistress of Dr Claes.

But the sacrilege was not quite complete; there was another and an august figure that loomed behind Julius de Coster Junior and his 'charming wife' – the venerable Founder of the House, de Coster Senior, who, for all his eighty-three years, still presided daily in his gloomy sanctum, dispensing high command. His son now said:

'I bet you haven't a notion how that old ruffian of a father of mine made his fortune. It was during the Boer War. He shipped to South Africa all the dud munitions he could buy from armament factories in Germany and Belgium. Now he's completely gaga; one has to guide the pen when he signs his name . . . Another bottle, landlord! Now do finish that drink, my dear Mister Popinga. Tomorrow, if you feel like it, you can repeat to our worthy fellow-townsmen every word I've spoken. For tomorrow I shall be dead – officially.'

By this time Kees was certainly quite drunk; all the same, he didn't miss a single word or change of expression on his employer's face. Only it seemed to him that the conversation was taking place in a dream-world, and that once he stepped out into the street he would be back in the world of real life.

'Really, what worries me most about it all is – you! Still, let me remind you that it was you who insisted on investing all your savings in the firm. If I'd refused to let you, you'd have been vexed. And you've only yourself to blame if you chose to build a house on the twenty-years' credit plan, with the result that, if you fail to pay your next instalment –'

He paused, and gave dramatic proof of his complete lucidity by asking:

'The next instalment's due on the thirty-first of this month, isn't it?' He seemed genuinely distressed.

'I assure you, I did what I could. Only the luck was dead against me. It was a deal in sugar put the lid on it – and I'd rather make a fresh start from zero than stay here to fight it out with all those pompous skunks of Groningen. Sorry! Present company excepted, needless to say. You're a good sort, and you weren't brought up as they were. Here's luck, Popinga my boy!'

This time he'd omitted the 'Mister'!

'Take my word for it, the people here aren't worth the trouble one takes to keep in their good books. Damned hypocrites, the lot of them! They expect you to behave like a plaster saint, while everyone of them is out to pick his neighbour's pocket. I've no wish to distress you, but I can't help thinking of your daughter, whom I happened to see last week. Well, between ourselves, she's so unlike you, with her dark hair and dreamy eyes, that I really wonder if you're her father ... Anyhow, when all is said and done, what the hell does it matter? Or, rather, what would it matter if one had the guts to break the rules oneself? It's when one persists in playing the game that one's had for a mug.'

He was no longer talking for Popinga's benefit, but for himself. After a short pause he summed up:

'Yes, the wisest thing is to be the first to break the rules. That way one's sure of not being "had". And what is one risking? Precious little really. Tonight I'm going to place Julius de Coster's clothes on the canal bank. Tomorrow everyone will think I've drowned myself. Death rather than dishonour! And the damned fools will spend heaven knows how many florins dragging the canal. But long before that I'll be well away with the twelve-five train. Listen, Popinga!'

Kees gave a start, as if waking from a dream.

'Now, if you're not too drunk, try to follow what I say. And, above all, don't run away with the idea I'm trying to bribe you. Nothing's farther from my mind, and, if I've told you all this it's because I know you'd never dream of repeating a word of it to anyone. That's so, isn't it? Right! Now I'll try to put myself in your shoes. Actually you haven't a penny in the world, and from what I know of the building society you deal with they'll make no bones about grabbing your house when you default on the next instalment. Your wife will be furious with you. Everyone will think you were my accomplice. You may find another job, or you may not, in which case you'll be up against it – like your brother-in-law. I've a thousand florins in my pocket. If you stay here, I can do nothing for you. Five hundred florins won't see you far. But if during the next twenty-four hours you come to your senses . . . There you are, old chap.'

Kees was amazed to see him push across the table half the little pile of banknotes.

'Take 'em. And there's something more. I still have a few irons in the fire. I'll be on my feet again one of these days. Now listen well! There's a paper I've been reading for the last thirty-five years, and shall continue reading as long as it appears. It's the *Morning Post*. If you decide to leave this god-forsaken town and if you're in difficulties of any kind, just put a message signed *Kees* in the Personal Column. That'll do the trick. Now will you come and . . . see me off? I hated the idea of clearing out like a poor devil on his beam-ends without anyone to say goodbye to me. What do I owe you, landlord?'

He paid the bill, picked up his parcel by the string and seemed glad to see that his companion could walk comparatively straight.

'We'll keep to the darker streets. Now, think it over, Popinga. Tomorrow I'll be dead – and that's the best thing that can happen to a man.'

As they walked past the 'fun house', Kees felt no reaction whatever; he was too much engrossed in his thoughts and the problem of keeping his balance. In a vain access of politeness he made as if to relieve his employer of the brown-paper parcel, but was waved away.

'Let's take this street. It's quieter.'

There was nobody about. All Groningen was asleep – except at the Saint George, the 'fun house', and the railway station.

What followed was like a dream. They had made their way to the bank of the Wilhelmina Canal, not far from one of the *Eleanores* – the *Eleanore IV*, which was loading cheese for Belgium. The snow was hard as ice. Instinctively Kees gave his employer his arm as he walked to the edge of the canal and deposited the clothes from the parcel at the water's edge. He had a momentary glimpse of the famous hat, but he didn't feel like smiling . . .

'And now, if you're not too sleepy, you might come to the station and see the last of me. I've taken a third-class ticket.'

It was a typical night-train, grimed and somnolent, aban-doned at the end of the platform while the station-master in an orange-coloured cap stood by, waiting to blow his whistle before going to bed.

Some Italians – what were they doing here? – could be seen recumbent amongst piles of shapeless bundles in one of the carriages, and, preceded by two porters, a young man in a frieze overcoat stepped haughtily into a first-class compartment, then took off his gloves to fish in his pockets for a tip.

'How about coming with me?'

De Coster said it laughingly, but Kees felt his heart miss a beat. Despite his potations, or perhaps because of them, things which had once seemed dark were now as clear as daylight, and he had half a mind to tell . . . No, the moment wasn't propitious – and, anyhow, he needed time to work out his programme. Moreover, de Coster might think he was showing off.

'It's rotten luck for you, old chap. I'm sorry. Still, such is life. Don't forget about that message in the Personal Column. Not too soon, though; I'll need a little time to . . .'

A sort of haze came over Kees as the train drew out, gathering speed with little jerks, and never could he remember how he got home that night, or how for the last time he saw shadows moving on a blind – of the second floor this time – of the 'fun house', or how, when he reached home, he managed to undress without Mum's noticing anything amiss.

Five minutes later the bed began to rock in a frightening rhythm, and Kees could only clutch desperately at the sheets, with a horrible sensation that at any moment he might be pitched out into the canal, whence the crew of *Ocean III* would not stir a finger to rescue him.

2

How Kees Popinga, though he had slept on the wrong side, woke in good form, and how he was hard put to choose between Eleanore and Pamela

Usually Kees slept badly if he chanced to lie on his left side. His breathing was laboured, there was a weight on his chest, and he groaned so loudly as to wake his wife, who promptly turned him over.

But after this memorable night, though he had slept on his left side, he couldn't remember having had a single disagreeable dream. And, what was stranger still, he woke up feeling completely lucid – whereas usually it was a struggle to get his mind to march again.

What awoke him, without his having to trouble to open his eyes, was a light creak of the bed-springs, signifying that his wife was getting up. On ordinary days this was a signal to Kees to doze off again with a clear conscience, knowing he had a good half-hour in hand.

But today things were different. And, when his wife was out of bed and, standing in front of the looking-glass, taking out her hairpins, he even opened a cautious eye to contemplate her.

She had no idea she was being watched, and moved as quietly as she could, to avoid waking her husband. Then she went into the bathroom and switched on the light; the door stood ajar and Kees had occasional glimpses of her.

The man had not yet come down the street to turn off the gaslamps, but there was a rhythmic sound of scraping; the snow was being shovelled away. Downstairs, the maid, whom they had never succeeded in persuading to work quietly, seemed to be engaged in a pitched battle with her stove and saucepans.

Mum put on her flannel knickers, clasped with elastic bands above the knees, and in this attire walked about the bathroom, cleaning her teeth, spitting with a strange grimace and performing her elaborate morning routine, without a notion she was being observed.

In the boy's room an alarm clock shrilled, and more sounds followed from that quarter, while Kees, lying on his back, calmly decided not to get up.

That was his first big decision of the day. He saw no point in getting up, since the House of Julius de Coster was bankrupt! He smiled as he pictured his wife's reaction when he announced that he was determined to stay in bed!

Too bad! She had other shocks coming, poor old Mum!

Thinking of Mum, Kees remembered a talk they once had had, that now was all too apposite. One day, five years previously, he had bought a mahogany row-boat that he christened the *Zeedeufel*, otherwise 'Sea-devil', and really, without the least exaggeration, one couldn't wish for a handsomer little craft; it had shapely lines, elegant brass fittings, and was always kept so spick and span that it would have looked more at home in a showcase than on the water.

Naturally it had cost a large sum, and its acquisition had gone to Kees's head. On the evening of the day he paid for it he had settled down complacently to taking stock of his possessions: house, furniture, linen, silver plate . . .

That evening he and his wife had been so convinced of their prosperity that in joking mood they had started discussing what they'd do if they woke one morning to find themselves ruined.

'I've thought about it sometimes,' said Mum with her usual quiet gravity. 'The first thing would be to sell all we have and send the children to good, cheap boarding schools. You, Kees, would certainly find a job on a ship. As for me, I'd go to Java and try to get a place as storekeeper at an hotel. You remember Maria's aunt, the one who lost her husband? That's what she did, and I gather she has a very good social position out there, not to mention a well-paid job.'

He all but laughed aloud. 'And now it's really happened! We *are* ruined! So it's up to her to go to Java and start counting sheets and napkins in a big hotel.'

Really, of course, it only showed what nonsense one talks when making plans against improbable disaster. For, to start with, the house would be seized and all their goods sold up. And, in the prevailing depression, his chances of getting engaged as a ship's officer were negligible.

In any case, Kees hadn't the least wish to go to sea. Had anyone asked him at that moment what he really desired, his answer would have been: 'Eleanore de Coster, or else Pamela.'

For, in the chaos of his memories of the previous night, the two women held the foreground. Eleanore in her silk dressing-gown, with her long jade cigarette-holder, coils of dark hair bunched on the whiteness of her neck. (To think she was the mistress of Dr Claes, a friend of his, with whom he often played chess!) And Pamela, at Amsterdam, who, when Julius de Coster wanted to play the viceroy, called in other girls to help to entertain him.

The frost-flowers on the panes were whitening with the dawn. The small boy had gone downstairs and must be having his breakfast, as his school began at eight. Frida, slower and more methodical, like her mother, was tidying up her bedroom.

'It's half-past seven, Kees.'

Mum had to repeat it twice before he deigned to answer, yawning and stretching himself:

'Shan't get up this morning.'

'Feeling ill?'

'No, but I shan't get up.'

He was in a larky mood and, fully aware how the remark must strike her, mischievously relished the look of consternation on his wife's face as she approached the bed.

'Whatever is the matter, Kees? Aren't you going to the office today?'

'No.'

'Have you let Mr de Coster know?'

'No.'

The queerest thing was that his present attitude wasn't in the least affected; it came quite naturally. This, in fact, was how he should always have behaved!

'Listen, Kees! You're not properly awake. It's time to be getting up . . . If you're ill, why not tell me so frankly, instead of frightening me over nothing?'

'I'm not ill, and I'm staying in bed. Would you have some tea sent up, please?'

Even de Coster would never have guessed the truth. He'd imagined that his revelations would strike Kees with dismay – but Kees didn't feel in the least dismayed. The only thing that came as a surprise was the discovery that someone else – and that someone else his employer, of all people! – should have had the same ideas as he – or, rather, the same dreams, for in Kees's case all that had never got beyond the stage of daydreams.

That feeling about trains, for instance. Of course he had long outgrown the boyish glamour of the steam-engine. Yet there was something that had an appeal for him in trains, especially in night-trains, which always put queer, vaguely improper notions into his head – though he would have been hard put to it to define them. Also he had an impression that those who leave by night-trains leave for ever – especially when he saw poor families crammed together with their bundles in the third-class carriages. Like those Italians the night before.

In fact, Kees Popinga had often and often dreamt of being someone quite different from the Kees Popinga everybody knew. That was why he always tended to overplay his part, out-Popinga'd Popinga, so to speak – for he knew that, were he to give way on the smallest point, there were no lengths to which he mightn't go.

At night, particularly. When Frida started her homework, and Mum was pasting pictures in her album, and he was fumbling with the wireless, puffing his cigar in the overheated room – how often had he had an impulse to stand up and say right out:

'Family life is a damned bore!'

It was to keep himself from saying or even thinking it that he stared at the stove, telling himself it was the finest stove in Holland, and Mum a pearl amongst women, and his daughter a fascinating child with those big brown dreamy eyes!

Passing by the 'fun house', too ... Very likely if he had entered it just once it would have been the turning-point. He'd have taken boldly to the primrose path, kept a pretty lady like Pamela, sampled many species of forbidden fruit – for his imagination ranged farther than de Coster's ...

The street door opened and shut; there was the tinkle of a bicycle bell. Karl was starting off to school. In a quarter of an hour it would be Frida's turn ...

'Here's your tea. It's nice and hot. Are you quite sure, Kees, you aren't ill?'

'Quite sure.'

A moment later he realized that this had been an over-statement. So long as he lay motionless in bed he had felt no physical discomfort of any kind. But no sooner did he sit up to drink his tea than there was a stab of pain in his neck and his head began to swim.

'You're looking pale. I'm sure something's wrong. Was there any bother about the *Ocean III*?'

'Bother? None at all.'

'Won't you tell me what's the trouble, Kees?'

'All right, I will. I'm sick of all this bloody fuss you're making, and I want to be left in peace.'

It was as outrageous as had been the sight of Julius de Coster in the Saint George tavern. Never had such words been uttered in the house; they were enough to make it rock to its foundations. And the curious thing was that he had uttered them not in anger but in quite an ordinary tone, the tone in which he would have asked for another cup of tea or a lump of sugar.

'Now, Mum, will you be very nice and not ask any more questions. I'm forty, and I don't see why I shouldn't be allowed to manage things in my own way – for a change.'

She couldn't bring herself to leave; after settling the pillow behind his head she halted halfway to the door and shot a piteous glance at him. At last the door closed soundlessly behind her.

'I bet she's going to have a cry,' thought Kees, hearing her stop again on the landing.

It was a queer sensation being in bed at that hour of the morning, on a day that wasn't Sunday. He heard Frida leave, and then a new experience began for him, for sounds came to his ears that he had never heard before: the milkman delivering the milk, the rooms downstairs being cleaned – domestic events of which he had known till now only by hearsay.

Undoubtedly the more alluring of the two was Eleanore. But against that was the fact that he hardly felt in her league. Though, of course, he was as good a man as Dr Claes, any day! He, Kees, was of the same age as the doctor, and regularly beat him at chess. What was more, Claes smoked a pipe, and very few women like that.

With Pamela it would be easier going. Especially now that he knew ... Incredible that he'd never dared during the two years that she lived in Groningen!

Something had just occurred to him and, getting out of bed, he walked barefoot across the linoleum carpet. The twinges in the back of his head and his dizziness were worse than ever.

He wanted to make sure his wife hadn't carried off his coat to brush it, for in that case she'd turn out the pockets and find the five hundred florins.

The coat was hanging on the back of a chair. Kees took the notes out of a pocket, slipped them under the pillow, and nearly went to sleep again in the warm bed.

Yes, it had better be Pamela . . . Why had de Coster pointed out that his daughter Frida was dark and not like him at all? It was true enough. But it was hard to imagine someone like Mum cheating on him from the very first year of their marriage! And hadn't there been lots of dark people in the Netherlands ever since the Spanish occupation? And don't hereditary traits sometimes skip several generations?

Anyhow – what did he care? Yes, that would have amazed Julius de Coster, who had fancied his cynicism was impressing Kees. He simply didn't care a damn! Once he had ceased to be a managing clerk and his house was his no longer; once a single detail had been changed, the whole caboodle might go phutt for all he cared! Yes, he was quite prepared to smoke a pipe like Claes, to eat third-grade cheese, to order gin at all the *vergüning* taverns in the town without a blush!

An early sunbeam fell aslant the room, filtering through a spotted-net curtain and ending in a blur of light on the looking-glass. Kees could hear the two women at work downstairs, moving pails and floorcloths; now and again, he suspected, his wife would cock an ear ceilingwards, to hear if he was getting up.

A ring at the bell. A whispered conversation in the hall. Mrs Popinga tramped upstairs, entered the bedroom with an apologetic air, and said uncomfortably:

'A man has come for the key.'

The key of the de Coster building obviously. He pictured them waiting at the entrance door, lost in wild conjectures.

'Right-hand pocket of my coat.'

'Haven't you any message for him to take?'

'None whatever.'

'You won't send a note to Mr de Coster?'

'No.'

Never could he have believed it of himself. This present mood was something beyond his wildest fancies. If proof were needed he had only to recall that time they had toyed with the idea of being ruined, when all they had thought up was such absurd plans as storekeeping in a Java hotel for his wife and, for himself, a second mate's berth on a steamer.

Absurd indeed! No half-measures for him, now that ruin was reality! Since the past was dead and done with, the only thing to do was to make the most of his new freedom.

He even regretted having missed the chance of telling de Coster on the previous evening how he felt about it. He'd let the man rattle on, and probably take him for a fool, or anyhow a weakling, incapable of deciding for himself – though his decision was already made! Yes, he should have said bluntly to his employer:

'Do you know what I'm going to do, to start with? I'm going to look up Pamela, in Amsterdam.'

It was an old account he was settling. Not very serious, perhaps, on the face of it, but it took precedence over all else. For what humiliated Kees most was the fact that he had never dared: that week after week he had walked past a certain house, blushing like a nasty-minded schoolboy, while . . . Well, anyhow, that was settled. Pamela to begin with; after that he'd see . . .

He'd see. If Kees had no idea of what he meant to do, he had a very clear idea of what he didn't mean to do. That was another thing he hadn't had the nerve to say on the previous evening, when the subject had cropped up, on two occasions actually.

Hadn't de Coster mentioned Arthur Merkemans? And hadn't Claes, too, referred to him, as if to say:

'Your brother-in-law's been round sponging on me again. What a rotter that chap is!'

Kees was quite decided not to become another Merkemans. He was in a good position to know how things stood in Groningen. Hardly a week passed but fellows with better qualifications than himself came round touting for a job, any sort of job. And the most revolting was the man who had well-cut, if threadbare, clothes, and groaned:

'I was managing director at Messrs So-and-so. But I've a wife and children, and I'll take any post you have to offer.'

They went from door to door, attaché-cases under their arms, trying to sell vacuum-cleaners or life-insurance policies.

'No,' Kees said aloud, staring at his distant reflection in the glass.

He wouldn't wait till his suits were shabby, his shoes in holes, and his friends at the chess club so touched by his misfortunes as to refrain from asking for his subscription – as had once been done for one of the members, with a vote by the committee, parade of noble sentiments, and the rest of it.

No, that way out was definitely not for him. True, he could never have gone so far as to bring about deliberately what had happened. Still, as it *had* happened, why not make the most of it?

'What do you want now?' he shouted.

'Mrs de Coster wants to know if you can give her any news of her husband. It seems he didn't come home last night, and . . .'

'What the hell has that to do with me?'

'Shall I tell her you don't know anything?'

'Tell her to go to the devil – and take her boyfriend with her.'

Whereat Mrs Popinga wondered if she were standing on her heels or on her head.

'Please be good enough to see my door is kept shut. And tell the maid not to make all that damned noise with her bucket.'

He noticed his head was aching and, calling his wife back, asked for an orange, for his mouth was gummed up and his tongue felt twice its normal size.

The sunbeam widened. He guessed that out of doors the air was keen, invigorating, and he could hear the noises of the harbour, the whistles of boats approaching the first bridge over the canal and asking to be let through. Was *Ocean III* still alongside? He supposed she was. The skipper would have ordered his oil from one of the rival firms, Wrichten most likely, who must be wondering what it meant.

At the office the staff must be scratching their heads and waiting for him to appear.

So then – he enjoyed summing up his programme – Pamela, to start with. De Coster had told him she had a suite at the Carlton Hotel. After that, with his five hundred florins, he'd take a train, a night-train, needless to say – why not the luxurious *Étoile du Nord*?

How long would it be before they found de Coster's clothes? There was a man who sold fishing-tackle near the place where they were lying. That black hat would show up against the snow.

'Now look here, Mum! If you disturb me again, I shall . . .'

'Kees! A perfectly dreadful thing has happened. Your boss has drowned himself.'

'You don't say so! Anyhow, why should it bother *me*?'

As he spoke he watched himself in the glass to make sure his face was absolutely impassive. It had always been one of his favourite amusements, posing before a looking-glass, striking one attitude after another and studying the effect.

Perhaps, at bottom, he had been cut out for an actor and it

29

was a part he had been playing for the last fifteen years, the part of a worthy, rather stolid Dutchman, well pleased with himself and convinced not only of his own immense respectability but of the high quality of everything he possessed.

'How can you talk that way, Kees? Or didn't you understand what I said? Julius de Coster has drowned himself.'

'Well, what about it?'

'Really, you'll make me think you knew something . . .'

'What do you expect me to do? Burst into tears because a man's committed suicide?'

'But he's . . . he's your employer, and . . .'

'He was free to do as he pleased, wasn't he? Now didn't you hear me say I wanted to sleep? So I'll ask you to leave me in peace.'

'How can I? There's one of the staff downstairs, and he insists on seeing you.'

'Tell him I'm asleep.'

'I expect the police will be coming, too, to ask you questions.'

'Very likely. I'll get up when they come – and not before.'

'Kees, you frighten me! There's something wrong with you. Your eyes look so strange . . .'

'Will you have some cigars sent up, please?'

By now she was convinced her husband was really ill, or anyhow sickening for something, and perhaps not quite in his right mind. In a resigned tone she told the servant to take a box of cigars upstairs, for it seemed wisest to humour him in his present mood. She had a long, whispered conversation with the man in the hall; finally he went away with a dejected air.

'Aren't you feeling well, sir?' the servant asked dutifully on entering the bedroom.

'Not feeling well? I've never felt better in my life. Who said I was ill?'

'The missus, sir.'

It was now about ten, Kees supposed, and a dozen or more

ships were busily discharging cargo down in the docks. He couldn't help feeling sorry to be missing the scene, which on this sunny morning must be a feast of colour as most of the ships had red, green, or blue sheer-strakes which were reflected in the water, and some of them would be taking advantage of the fine day to dry their sails.

He had often watched them from his office window. He knew all the skippers, all the watermen. And he knew, too, the distinctive note of every ship's siren, and could announce in advance:

'That's the *Jesus-Maria* passing the second bridge. She'll be here in half an hour.'

Then on the stroke of eleven the office-boy would bring him a cup of tea and two biscuits.

Meanwhile de Coster Senior sat in his sanctum, all by himself, behind heavily padded baize doors. Queer that no one had suspected that the old man was gaga! Every morning he was packed into an armchair like a mummy – or like the House figurehead. No interview with him lasted more than a minute or so, and customers took his mindless gaze and silence for tokens of profound sagacity.

The bed was getting clammy and Kees kept shifting his position. His pyjama sleeves were sticking under his arms. But he couldn't bring himself to get up, for, once up, he'd have to start really doing things.

So long as he stayed in bed he could do them in imagination, and Pamela seemed quite accessible. Even Eleanore de Coster, cigarette-holder and all, failed to daunt him! But it would be another matter when he had got into his grey suit and was standing in front of his mirror, washed and shaved, his fair hair plastered down with brilliantine.

Already he was finding trouble in struggling against his curiosity – not to mention another less definite feeling – and a desire to go to the office and take a hand in the extraordinary things that must be happening there. The skipper of *Ocean III*, a tough customer at the best of times, would certainly be on the warpath and threatening a suit for damages.

And suppose the police did visit the office? A visit from the police would rattle the staff badly, and he wondered how it would go off. All the ground floor consisted of storerooms filled roof-high with merchandise of all descriptions, with blue-aproned warehousemen in attendance. In one corner was an office with windows on all sides, one of which overlooked the docks and the others the storeroom. This was the managing clerk's office, and in it Kees played the part of leader of the orchestra.

On the first floor were smaller storerooms and some offices, while on the second floor, above the six-foot signboard blazoned with the firm's name, *Julius de Coster and Son, Ship-chandler*, were still more offices.

He was brave enough to stay in bed but, though he himself had given the order that he was not to be disturbed, he felt vexed at being left so long in solitude.

What were they up to, the two women downstairs? Why couldn't he hear them moving now? And why didn't anyone come to question him about his employer's suicide?

He would give nothing away, of course. Still, this lack of eagerness to question him was like a slight.

He ate his orange without a knife and threw the peel on the floor, just to vex Mum; then snuggled down again between the sheets, burying his head deep in the pillow, shut his eyes, and forced his thoughts on to Pamela and the things they'd do together.

The whistle of a train pleasantly jogged his memory, and in a half-dream he recalled his decision not to leave in the daytime – that would be too humdrum – but take a night-train, or anyhow one that left after nightfall, which came at about four.

Pamela, like Eleanore, was a brunette; she was plumper than Mrs de Coster. His wife was buxom, but you wouldn't call her plump. She always showed signs of confusion when at night Kees was in an amorous mood, and started at the least sound, for she was always in terror the children might 'hear something'.

Though Kees tried to fix his mind on Pamela to the exclusion of all else, pictures kept rising before him of the de Coster office, of sunlit corners of the docks, ships loading and discharging cargo. Impatiently he rolled himself over in the bed, and started off again:

'When I enter her room at the Carlton, I'll say to her . . .' And proceeded to con over, minute by minute, the sequence of events as he foresaw it.

'Papa!'

He must have gone really asleep, for he sat bolt upright with a jerk and gazed bemusedly at his daughter, who whimpered:

'What have you been doing to Mum?'

'What do you mean?'

'She's crying, and she says you're not yourself, and all sorts of dreadful things are happening.'

Very smart of her!

'Where is she now – your mother?'

'In the dining-room. Karl's back from school and we're just going to start dinner. Mum didn't want me to come upstairs.'

Frida had a knack of waxing lachrymose without actually shedding tears. As quite a small child she would continue snivelling for hours as if she were a victim of the most horrible ill-treatment. The least thing was enough to set her off: from a quite innocuous remark to the mere hint of a frown. She got into this state so frequently and with such ease that one could never be sure if she was really unhappy at such moments.

'Mr de Coster's dead, isn't he?'

'He may be for all I care!'

'Mum says you're ill.'

'Does she now?'

'Yes, and she wants to call in Dr Claes, only she's afraid you might be angry.'

'And so I should be. I don't need Claes, or anyone else.'

What a queer girl! Kees had never been able to make her out, and just now, as she stood at the bedside, gazing at him with big scared eyes, she baffled him more than ever. What could be at the back of her mind? And, oddly enough, with all her plaintiveness, she had a marvellous gift for coming back to realities.

'What shall I tell Mum? Shall I say you're coming down to dinner?'

'I shan't come down.'

'Shall we have it without you?'

'That's just what you'll do. And you can all have a good cry together, into the soup, if you feel like it ... And now, for God's sake, leave me in peace!'

His conscience didn't prick him, but he felt he had handled the situation clumsily. He'd have done far better to leave the house at the normal hour and let them think he was going to the office.

As it was, he couldn't quite decide what line to take, and he foresaw endless complications. Not the least infliction would be a visit from his brother-in-law, Merkemans, who never missed an opportunity of this kind for butting in with a great show of devotion and offers to help in any way he could. Whenever there was a death in the neighbourhood, he never failed to volunteer to keep vigil by the corpse.

'Now go downstairs, Frida, and have your dinner. Didn't I tell you I wanted to be left alone?'

What he needed to set him up was a glass or two of gin. But there was no alcoholic drink in the house, except a bottle of bitters, kept for emergencies, when somebody dropped in unexpectedly. And, anyhow, the bottle was locked up in the sideboard cellaret.

'Bye-bye, Frida.'

'Bye-bye, Papa.'

She failed to notice that he had spoken, involuntarily, in a different tone from his usual one, and that he followed her with his eyes as she walked out of the room. No sooner was the door closed than he buried his head again in the pillow. But he was conscious of gradually losing grip and finding it harder and harder to keep his thoughts on Pamela and the rest of it.

Luckily a message was brought to him at two, to inform him that the police were holding an inquiry at the de Coster building and required his presence immediately.

He dressed with extreme care and studied himself lengthily in the glass. When he came down he kept hovering round his wife – which emboldened her to ask:

'Don't you think it might be better if I came with you?'

That settled it. His resolution had been weakening again, but the fact that somehow she had sensed impending danger and was taking steps to counter it clinched the matter.

'Thanks,' he said gruffly. 'I'm quite old enough to handle matters of that sort without your help.'

Her eyes were red, and so was her nose, as always when she had been crying. She didn't dare to meet his gaze – a sure sign she had something at the back of her mind.

'Are you taking your bike, dear?'

'No.'

She seldom called him 'dear' nowadays; only on special occasions.

'Why are you crying?' he asked fretfully.

'I'm not crying.'

She might say it, but the tears were streaming down her cheeks.

'Silly fool!' he murmured under his breath.

A remark she was never to understand; nor would she ever realize there was more affection in it than in anything he had ever said to her.

'You won't be too late coming back?'

The most ridiculous thing was that he, too, was on the brink of tears. The five hundred florins were in his pocket. But he had left behind the two hundred kept in a drawer in his room to meet a bill that would be presented in two days' time.

'Got your gloves, dear?'

No, he was forgetting his gloves. She went and fetched them. She didn't kiss him – that was not their way – but she lingered in the doorway for some moments, leaning forward to watch his receding figure and listening to the crunch of his galoshes on the snow.

It was all he could do to resist a temptation to look back.

3

Concerns a notebook, bound in red leather, which Kees had bought for a florin, after winning a chess tournament

A quarter of an hour had passed since the train had left Groningen. As it was half-past four and already quite dark, there wasn't the resource of looking out of the windows. Two other passengers were in the second-class compartment with Kees: a wispy little man who looked like a bailiff or a lawyer's clerk and, in the opposite corner, a middle-aged woman in widow's weeds.

Kees put his hand in his coat pocket and his fingers lit on a small book. It was a notebook, bound in red morocco and gilt-edged, which he had bought for a florin with the intention of recording in it games of chess that had interested him. So far only two pages of the book had been employed; covered, that is to say, with the cabalistic signs used by chess players.

When he took it from his pocket, he had no particular idea in mind. Then something moved him to draw the pencil from its sheath in the binding and write on a blank page: '*Left Groningen by the 4.7 p.m. train.*'

He put the notebook back in his pocket. Some time later, as the train was leaving Sneek station, he took it out again and wrote: '*Too short a stop to get out for a drink.*'

A day would come when that notebook and those entries were adduced by mental specialists to prove that, from the time of leaving Groningen, he was insane! And yet – was his wife mad because she persisted in keeping up the diary she had started as a girl, and of an evening, when there were no flower pictures to paste in her album, would record in all seriousness: '*Bought a pair of shoes for Karl. Frida went to the hairdressers*'?

As a matter of fact, it wasn't only the notebook that the doctors had to go on. His fellow-passengers, though at the time they hardly glanced at Kees, were to declare with one accord that they had noticed several queer things about him, and back their statements up with details.

Yet really there was nothing in his demeanour to draw attention to him. He was quite calm; perhaps exaggeratedly so. He himself noticed this, and it brought to his mind two incidents in his past life when he had displayed the same involuntary *sang-froid*.

It was the red notebook that recalled the first of these two incidents, for it centred round a game of chess. One evening at the club he had won three games running, and old Copenghem, who for some reason had his knife into Popinga, had sneered:

'It's easy winning when one only takes on players weaker than oneself.'

Bitterly offended, Kees had made a sharp retort. Then they had come to challenging each other, and finally Kees had offered to take on Copenghem with a rook and a bishop short.

That game had remained memorable in the annals of the club, and Kees recalled every detail. Though Copenghem was an excellent player, Kees professed to be quite sure of winning and, what was more, deliberately infuriated his opponent by getting up and strolling round the room between the moves. On a low table beside him was a tankard of Munich beer, a barrel of which had just been delivered at the club.

After an hour's play, during which Kees never ceased making ironical, not to say offensive, remarks, Copenghem mated him.

The defeat was all the more exasperating for Kees as some twenty members of the club had gathered round to watch the game, and they had heard him bragging.

Nevertheless he didn't turn a hair; neither paled nor flushed. On the contrary, a preternatural calm came over him and he remarked airily:

'Well, these things happen, don't they?'

At the same moment his hand closed, unperceived, on one of the chessmen: a bishop. It was an ivory set, famed in the Groningen chess world; it belonged to Copenghem, who declared it put him off his game to play with any other.

It was the black bishop he was holding. He had worked out the plan in a flash, and a moment later dropped it into his tankard of beer.

Another game was just about to start. The absence of the bishop was discovered, and everybody, including the waiter, set to hunting for it high and low. All sorts of theories were put forward, but no one gave a thought to the tankard of brown beer that Kees was careful not to drink. Nor was the mystery ever solved, and Copenghem never saw his bishop again.

While the search was going on, Kees had experienced the same sensation of blissful calm that he now felt in the railway carriage, thinking of the good folk of Groningen on whom he'd played another vanishing trick.

None the less, the elderly lady in black was to declare two days later:

'He had a crazy look in his eyes, and once or twice I saw him laughing to himself.'

'Laughing' was too strong; he merely grinned – the first time on recalling the Copenghem episode, the second time the episode of the oxtail soup.

The latter was more recent. It had taken place in the previous year at a big dinner-party given by Jef van Duren to celebrate his nomination to a professorship at the Faculty of Medicine. While vermouth was being handed round before dinner, Kees had slipped away to the kitchen, for Maria, the maid-of-all-work, was an attractive wench and he never missed a chance of flirting with her when visiting the van Durens.

But this time, no sooner did he risk a first caress than she rounded on him.

'You ought to be ashamed of yourself, Mr Popinga. As you won't behave properly I'm off, and I shan't come back till you're out of my kitchen!' And stamped down to the cellar, where presumably she had work to do.

It was all the more humiliating as Maria was almost the only girl with whom Kees took such liberties, and every time he did so he felt hot all over.

Though the rebuff had cut him to the quick he kept quite calm, indeed unnaturally calm. And, as his eyes had fallen on the chessman, so now they fell on a saucepan of oxtail soup simmering on the range – a soup that the van Durens provided only on great occasions. A row of tins stood on a shelf, two of them inscribed *Salt*. He took down one of them and poured half its contents into the soup. After that he returned to the drawing-room with an air of perfect innocence.

The outcome was even funnier than he'd anticipated. For some reason, the tin marked *Salt* actually contained powdered sugar. For a minute or more the faces of the van Durens' guests were a study in bewilderment and consternation. Now and again someone took a cautious sip, trying to guess what had happened, but the mystery of the soup remained unsolved.

And now in the railway carriage his composure was of exactly the same order. At six o'clock when the train reached Stavoren he hadn't yet managed to have a drink, though he had been feeling thirsty for some time. And at Stavoren he had to hurry to the ferry-boat plying across the Zuider Zee.

Fortunately drinks were forthcoming on the ferry, and no sooner had he taken a seat than he beckoned to the steward and said quite tranquilly:

'Two glasses of gin, please.'

He asked for two because he intended to drink two glasses and there was no point in making the man do two trips instead of one. After all, on the previous day, hadn't de Coster insisted on having the bottle of gin left on the table, without the landlord's finding it unusual? That being so, what possessed the steward to declare subsequently:

'He looked a bit barmy and, would you believe it, he ordered two glasses of gin at the same time!'

After the forty-minute crossing he boarded the Amsterdam train at Enkhuizen, reaching Amsterdam a little after eight. During this last stage of the journey he shared the carriage with two cattle-dealers who talked shop all the way, occasionally casting suspicious glances in his direction as if they saw in him a business rival.

But no one, not even he, had the least inkling of the appalling celebrity that was to befall him only a few hours later. He was, as usual, in a grey suit. Without thinking, he had tucked under his arm the small attaché case he always took with him to the office.

On reaching Amsterdam he made straight for the Carlton with the same prompt decision as he had shown when dropping the chessman into the tankard and pouring the sugar into the oxtail soup.

'Is Miss Pamela in?'

There was nothing, absolutely nothing, to differentiate him from an ordinary caller, except perhaps his extreme calmness.

'What name shall I give, sir?' asked the uniformed porter.

'Mr Julius de Coster.'

The porter hesitated, eyed him for a moment, then said in a puzzled tone:

'But – excuse me, sir – you aren't Mr de Coster.'

'How do you know that?'

'Mr de Coster comes every week, and I know his face quite well.'

'How can you be sure there isn't another Mr de Coster?'

All the same, when the porter picked up the telephone receiver, he thought best to say:

'There's a gentleman here who says he's been sent by Mr de Coster. Shall I send him up?'

The lift-boy took no special notice of Kees as they shot up to the fourth floor.

Pamela, who was seated at her dressing-table brushing her hair, called 'Come in!' in a casual tone; then looked round, for, though she had heard the door open, the visitor hadn't said a word.

She saw Kees standing near the door, hat in hand, his attaché case under his arm, and said amiably:

'Won't you sit down?'

To which he answered:

'Thank you . . . No.'

They were in one of the hundred more or less identical furnished suites of which the Carlton in Amsterdam consists. A door stood ajar, giving a glimpse of a brilliantly lit bathroom. A flimsy evening frock sprawled across the bed.

'Has Mr de Coster sent you with a message? Excuse me if I go on with my dressing. I'm rather pressed for time. By the way, what is the time exactly?'

'Half past eight . . . There's no hurry.'

He laid his hat and attaché case on a table beside him, took off his overcoat and, watching himself in a mirror, conjured up a smile.

'I'm quite sure you don't remember me, but I often used to see you in Groningen. And perhaps I may add that for two years I was exceedingly keen on you. Well, last night we had a talk together, Julius de Coster and I, and I decided . . .'

'What on earth are you getting at?'

'Don't you understand? I've come to see you now because the position's quite different from what it was when you were living in Groningen . . .' He had come quite near her, so near as to make her feel ill at ease, but she went on brushing her dark brown hair. 'It would take too long to explain things. It comes to this: I've decided to spend an hour or so with you.'

When he left the hotel he was, if that were possible, still calmer. He had not rung for the lift, and walked down the four flights of stairs. Only when he was on the ground floor did he realize he'd left his attaché case in Pamela's room.

As he was wondering whether the porter would notice this, he saw the man's gaze directed on his empty hands.

'Silly of me!' he said breezily. 'I left my attaché case upstairs. I'll call in for it tomorrow morning.'

'Wouldn't you like me to send a page up for it, sir?'

'No, don't bother. I shan't be needing it today.'

He made only one blunder, due to his unfamiliarity with the ways of luxury hotels; he took a small silver coin from his pocket and handed it to the porter.

Ten minutes later he was at the station. He had almost two hours to wait before the next express to Paris, which left at 11.26, and he spent the time strolling up and down the platforms and looking at the trains as they came in.

At a quarter to eleven a young woman, whose second string was dancing at a cabaret, and who was always to be seen about with Pamela at night, inquired of the Carlton porter:

'Hasn't she come down yet? I've been waiting for her at a restaurant for the last hour.'

'I'll phone to her room.'

The porter rang three times without success, then scratched his head.

'That's odd! Perhaps she's fallen asleep. I'm pretty sure she hasn't gone out.' He shouted to a passing page boy: 'Just run upstairs and see if Miss Pamela is in her room.'

On the platform Kees showed not the least sign of

impatience, and whiled away the time by studying the appearance of the people passing to and fro.

The page came racing down the stairs and slumped into a chair, yelling:

'Quick! Go up, somebody!'

He had abandoned the lift midway and they had to use the stairs. Pamela lay stretched across the bed, tightly gagged with a Turkish towel. The manager of the hotel was sent for, a doctor called in. By the time the police arrived it was half-past eleven and the Paris express had just left.

This train was the real thing, one of those night-expresses that had haunted Kees Popinga's imaginings – with sleeping-cars, dimmed lights and close-drawn blinds, and passengers speaking in various languages. More thrilling still, it was an international train and crossed two frontiers in the course of a few hours.

He was travelling second class and had found a carriage in which there was only one other passenger, a man lying full length on the seat, his face turned to the wall.

Kees felt no desire to sleep, or even to sit down, and he walked up and down the corridors, the full length of the train, three or four times. He walked slowly, peering into each carriage, trying to guess . . .

The guard punched his ticket without looking at him. The Belgian police officer merely glanced at his identity card. He took advantage of the customs inspection to jot down in his notebook:

'*Took the 23.26 at Amsterdam, second class.*' A few minutes later he was moved to add: '*Cannot make out why Pamela started laughing at me when I told her what I wanted. So much the worse for her, I couldn't let it go at that. By now, presumably, she understands.*'

If she had merely smiled, or made some sarcastic retort, he

might have let it pass. Or even if she'd lost her temper. But what she actually did was to go into peals of laughter that set her bosom heaving – and made her all the more alluring.

'Stop laughing!' he said angrily.

But that only made things worse. She laughed and laughed till the tears came to her eyes. He gripped her wrists.

'I forbid you to laugh. Do you hear?'

He thrust her roughly towards the bed; she fell back across it. As for the towel, it happened to be lying there to hand, beside the evening frock . . .

'Tickets, please!'

This time it was a Belgian guard, who, in spite of everything, cast a quizzical glance at this man standing out in the corridor despite the cold. But it was a long way from suspecting anything else . . .

The other man in the carriage had stirred a little when they crossed the frontier, and Kees had had a glimpse of a nondescript face, a small brown moustache.

A queer night, none the less, as thrilling in its way as the previous one, with de Coster airing his views in the Saint George! What would Julius Junior say when he heard the news?

Would Pamela lay a complaint? If so, his name would figure in the newspapers, as the attaché case left in her room contained clues to his identity.

Then practically anything might happen; in fact, he found it impossible to think out all the complications that would ensue. Take the case of Frida, for instance, who was in a convent school. Would they keep with them the daughter of a man who had . . . ? And what of the chess club? Copenghem would raise his hands in scandalized delight. And what a facer it would be for Dr Claes, who thought he was the only man in the town to dare to have a mistress!

He half closed his eyes. His face was quite expressionless. Sometimes through the window he saw a row of lights flash past, and sometimes the low rumble of the train swelled to a roar as they ran through a station. He had a glimpse of a vast snow-clad plain and of a little house where, though it was past midnight, the windows were lit up. Why should that be? Had someone died and were they keeping vigil?

He couldn't decide whether it was a good thing or not, his having left the attaché case behind in Pamela's room. Every moment he had an itch to write something more in the red notebook.

At the French frontier he got out of the train, ascertained that the buffet was open and, skirting the customs office, went to the bar and had a large glass of brandy. A moment later he scribbled in his notebook: '*Curious! Drink produces no effect at all on me!*'

The last stage of the journey was the longest. He had done his best to strike up an acquaintance with the other man in the carriage, a traveller for a firm of jewellers. But the man, who did the same journey twice a week, made a point of sleeping through it.

Nevertheless at one moment Kees tapped him on the shoulder, asking:

'Could you tell me if the Moulin Rouge will still be open when we get to Paris?'

He wanted to see people, and started roaming the corridors again, groping his way through the concertina-vestibules between the coaches, pressing his face to windows beyond which dim-lit figures swayed in uneasy attitudes of sleep.

If not the Moulin Rouge, some other place of the same sort. He had named the Moulin only because he'd heard so much about it.

Already he was picturing himself seated in an enormous room ablaze with lights and mirrors, with red-plush wall-sofas, a bottle of champagne on the table in front of him, and pretty ladies in extravagantly low-necked dresses at his side. But he would keep quite calm. The champagne would have no more effect on him than the gin and brandy he had drunk. And he'd get a mischievous pleasure out of passing remarks that the girls beside him couldn't understand.

Abruptly the picture faded and he found that he was standing on a draughty platform of the Gare du Nord, then walking to the Way Out, stepping into a taxi, saying to the driver:

'Take me to the Moulin Rouge.'

'No luggage, sir?'

'No.'

The Moulin Rouge was closed, but the taxi stopped outside another cabaret and a commissionaire sprang forward to open the door of the taxi. No one could have guessed that this was the first time in his life that he was entering an establishment of this sort. He showed no haste, took a good look round the room and, waving away the head waiter, strolled up to an empty table and sat down.

'Bring me a bottle of champagne and a cigar.'

So there he was! Everything had worked out according to plan, and it didn't surprise him in the least when a girl in a green dress came and sat beside him, smiling:

'OK?'

'Quite OK,' he replied.

'You're a foreigner, aren't you?'

'A Dutchman. But I speak three languages, French, English, and German, as well as my own.'

He felt extraordinarily pleased with himself. Once again everything, down to the least detail, was panning out exactly as he'd foreseen it. Almost he felt as if he had been here before, in this cabaret with the red-plush wall-sofas, a jazz band whose fair-haired saxophonist was certainly Nordic, perhaps a compatriot of his, and this red-haired girl who had planted her elbows on the table and was asking for a cigarette.

'Waiter!' he called. 'Cigarettes!'

After a few minutes he took the notebook from his pocket and asked the girl:

'What's your name?'

'My name? You want to write it down? What a funny idea! Well, I don't mind telling you, if you're so keen on it. Jeanne Rozier. By the way, it's almost closing time.'

'That's no matter.'

'Well, what do you propose to do?'

'Go to your place.'

'Sorry, nothing doing. To a hotel, if you like.'

'That'll be just as nice.'

'Well, I must say you're easily pleased.'

He had a tight smile; it was all so funny – though why, he didn't know. The girl asked casually:

'Do you often come to Paris?'

'It's the second time in my life. The first time was on my honeymoon.'

'Your wife with you this trip?'

'No, she's stayed at home.' He could hardly keep from laughing. Calling a waiter, he ordered another bottle of champagne. She tapped him lightly on the arm.

'You like the little girls, eh?'

This time he laughed outright.

'Not the "little" ones.' Of course, she couldn't know. But Pamela wasn't little; she was as tall as he. And Eleanore de Coster was a good five foot ten.

'Anyhow you're a cheerful sort, that's something! Are you in business?'

'I don't know yet.'

'What do you mean by that?'

'Oh, nothing . . . What a lot of freckles you have! It's awfully funny!'

What was funniest of all was to see how the girl kept shooting furtive glances at him, trying to size him up. She had freckles under her eyes, dully glowing red hair, a creamy-white complexion. Of the women he knew, only one was red-haired, the wife of one of the members of his chess club, and she was a tall, scraggy creature, mother of five.

'Why are you looking at me like that?'

'Oh, for no special reason. It's grand being in a place like this. Wouldn't Pamela be sick if she knew!'

'Who's Pamela?'

'Nobody you know.'

'I say, you'd better pay the waiter. I can see them all looking at us; they want to close down and go to bed.'

'Waiter! Will you change these florins, please?'

He took the five hundred from his pocket and handed them to the head waiter with an absentminded air. There was no denying it; he was tired. Indeed, at certain moments his one desire was to lie down and sleep; only it seemed preposterous to cut short a day like this by giving way to weariness.

'Why can't I spend the night at your place?'

'Because I've a . . . a friend.'

He looked at her suspiciously.

'What sort of fellow is he? Old?'

'He's thirty.'

'What's his job?'

'He's in business.'

'Oh, is he? I'm in business too.'

All the time he was observing himself, inwardly gloating over each remark he made, watching his gestures in a mirror on the wall facing him.

'Here you are, sir,' said the waiter airily.

But he took care to count the money carefully and remark:

'You've given too low a rate. I'd have had three points more in Amsterdam.'

As they stepped on to the pavement, Jeanne Rozier gazed steadily at him, as if weighing him up.

'What hotel are you staying at?'

'I'm not at an hotel. I came straight here from the station.'

'Where's your luggage then?'

'I haven't any.'

Again she hesitated. Wouldn't it perhaps be wiser to part company with him then and there? Surprised by her change of manner, Kees asked:

'What's wrong?'

'Nothing. Let's be off. I know quite a nice hotel in the Rue Victor-Massé. It's quite clean.'

There had been no snow in Paris, nor was it freezing. Kees felt as light and sparkling as the champagne he had been drinking. The girl walked into the hotel with the air of someone quite at home there, calling across a glazed door: 'Don't trouble to get up. We're going to Number Seven.'

She gave some final touches to the bed, bolted the door, and heaved a little sigh.

'Aren't you undressing?' she asked from the bathroom.

After all, why shouldn't he undress? He was ready to do whatever was expected of him; in the mood of a docile child who is being given a treat and is anxious to please everybody.

'Staying long in Paris?'

'Perhaps for ever.'

'Really? And you didn't bring any luggage . . . ?'

It was all so queer that by now she definitely regretted having got off with this fellow. Seated on the bed, Kees watched her undressing, with a flicker of amusement in his eyes.

'A penny for your thoughts,' she said.

'I was thinking that's a pretty chemise you're wearing. Real silk, isn't it?'

She kept it on as she slipped between the sheets and waited, leaving the light on.

'What are you up to?' she asked after a while.

'Nothing!'

He was merely finishing his cigar, lying on his back and gazing up at the ceiling.

'You're not . . . shy, by any chance?'

'No.'

'Mind if I turn the light off?'

'No.'

She switched it off, and in the darkness was still conscious of the man lying beside her, always in exactly the same attitude, his lips closed on the butt of his cigar, which emitted a dull red glow.

She was the first to make a move.

After shifting her position in the bed several times, she asked:

'Why did you get me to come here with you?'

'Don't you think it's nice here?'

He could feel the warmth of her body beside him, but the pleasure it gave him was purely mental, and he was smiling to himself. 'If only Mum were here . . . !'

Suddenly he sprang out of bed, turned on the light, went to his coat and fished out the notebook.

'What's the address?'

'The address of what?'

'This place we're at.'

'37A, Rue Victor-Massé. Do you really want to write it down?'

He did – much as some travellers want picture-postcards of the places they visit, or collect the menus of the restaurants they eat at. Then he came back to the bed, stubbed out his cigar-stump in the ashtray, and murmured:

'I don't feel sleepy yet . . . What sort of business is he in?'

'Who?'

'That friend of yours.'

'Oh, he's in the motor trade . . . But look here, if that's all you have to say, I'd rather you let me go to sleep. You're a queer bird and no mistake! What time shall I wake you up tomorrow?'

'You needn't wake me.'

'Good. I say, I hope you don't snore.'

'Only when I sleep on my left side.'

'Then try to sleep on your right side tonight.'

He remained awake, his eyes wide open, for a considerable time; to his amusement, it was the girl beside him who started snoring, like a steam-engine, and it was all he could do not to laugh out loud.

When he woke, the sun had risen but the curtains were still drawn to, so that only a thin ribbon of light passed between them, leaving half the room in darkness.

In many ways the scene was just like that in Groningen when, through half-closed eyes, he had watched Mrs Popinga dressing, unconscious of his gaze.

He saw Jeanne Rozier, fully dressed, outlined against the ray of light; she was holding his trousers with one hand while with the other she felt in the pockets. Evidently she had noticed when they were at the cabaret that he had thrust the wad of French banknotes into a trouser-pocket. So anxious was she not to make a sound that she was pursing her lips, and indeed looked so comical that Kees couldn't help smiling.

Some sixth sense must have apprised her of this smile, for suddenly she swung round towards him. Equally promptly he shut his eyes, so that she couldn't decide whether he was really asleep or only pretending.

It was amusing to know her standing there athwart the sunbeam, his trousers in her hand, holding her breath, not daring to make the least movement. For a moment she was taken in and her hand crept again towards a pocket; then, abruptly swinging round, she drawled:

'You there?'

'Eh?'

'Had enough of making a fool of me?'

'What do you mean?'

'That's all right! I've tumbled to it!' Dropping the trousers on to a chair, she took off her fur coat and planted herself beside the bed.

'Now you'd better come clean! I know why you came to Paris without any luggage, and with wads of money in your pocket. You had me on at first, but I've seen through your little game.'

'My little game? But –'

'Just a moment!' She walked to the window and flung back the curtains, flooding the room with cold grey light. 'Now – out with it!'

Sitting on the edge of the bed, she studied Kees's face attentively, then sighed:

'Yes, I was a fool not to spot you weren't the sort of chap who gets off with a girl just for the fun of it. When you talked about your "business" last night I should have tumbled to it. Anyhow, I've guessed what that "business" is, and I defy you to say I'm wrong . . . You're running dope.'

4

*How Kees Popinga spent
Christmas Eve, and how at
daybreak he chose a car*

The Carlton porter had taken him for a lunatic at large; now, because he showed no indignation on catching her going through his pockets, Jeanne Rozier took him for a dope-dealer! In a way, of course, it was rather a relief. For all these years it had been a strain playing the part of Kees Popinga, and watching himself incessantly to make sure he didn't say or do the wrong thing. Now all that was ended.

'I'm sleepy,' he murmured, without answering the girl, who was standing beside the bed and looking down at him.

In the greenish eyes flecked with small brown spots he could read more than mere curiosity. She was mystified and couldn't tear herself away before she'd solved the mystery. Placing one knee on the bed, she said tentatively:

'Suppose I got into bed again for a bit?'

'Don't bother!'

She still had in her hand the wad of notes taken from his pocket; ostentatiously she laid them on the bedside table.

'Look! There's your money ... You don't mind my taking one of these?'

He was awake enough to see it was a thousand-franc note she had selected. But it was all the same to him. He went to sleep again immediately.

Jeanne had only a couple of hundred yards to go in the brisk morning air. After mounting three flights of stairs, she entered her small furnished flat in the Rue Fromentin, closed the door soundlessly behind her, gave the cat a saucer of milk, then slipped out of her clothes and into a bed in which a man was lying.

'Shove up, Louis!'

He grunted something and made room for her.

'Do you know, I've just been with such a queer bird! He gave me the creeps.'

Louis showed no interest. After gazing for a quarter of an hour or so at the strip of light between the curtains, Jeanne too fell asleep: sound asleep this time, in her own bed, with the companionable warmth of Louis – who was wearing silk pyjamas – beside her.

At about the same time, as the offices began to fill up and people put off getting down to work by smoking their first, bitter-tasting cigarette of the day, a telegram from Amsterdam was handed in at the Sûreté Nationale of Paris:

> Man named Kees Popinga, age thirty-nine, resident of Groningen, wanted for murder of Pamela Mackinsen on night of 23 December in her suite at Carlton Hotel Amsterdam Stop Reasons to believe Popinga took train to Paris Stop Is wearing grey suit, grey felt hat Stop Fair hair, pale complexion, blue eyes, medium build, no distinguishing features Stop Speaks fluent English, German, French.

Promptly the smoothly running machinery of the Sûreté was set in motion; in other words, the description of Popinga was circulated by telegraph and telephone throughout France: to gendarmeries, frontier stations and headquarters of provincial Flying Squads. In each Paris police station a sergeant was taking down from the tape-machine: *'medium build, no distinguishing features'*.

Meanwhile, in the hotel bedroom Kees was indulging in an orgy of sleep. At midday the chambermaid tapped on the glazed door of the office, put her head in and inquired:

'Isn't Number Seven free yet?'

The manageress couldn't remember, so the girl went up to see. She found Kees still asleep, his mouth wide open, his face a picture of beatitude. On the bedside table was a little pile of banknotes, but she didn't dare to touch them.

It was four, and the lights had just been turned on, when Jeanne Rozier entered the hotel office.

'Has he gone yet, the fellow I was with last night?'

'I think he's still asleep.'

A newspaper in her hand, Jeanne went up the two flights of stairs, opened the door, and gazed intently at the man lying in the bed; his face had the innocent contentment of a sleeping child's.

Suddenly she called in a low voice:

'Kees!'

The sound had a faint echo in his dream, but had to be repeated several times before it reached his consciousness. Opening his eyes, he saw the lamp lit above his head and Jeanne in a squirrel coat, with her hat on, bending over him.

'Ah, you're still here,' he murmured vaguely; then began to roll over on to his other side to resume his interrupted dream. But she caught his shoulder and shook it.

'Didn't you hear what I said?'

He gazed at her absently, passed his hand over his eyes, and in a voice almost as childish as the expression on his face when he was sleeping, asked:

'What was it you said?'

'Your name . . . Kees . . . Kees Popinga.' She emphasized each syllable meaningly, but he showed no interest.

'Haven't you tumbled to it? Well, read this.'

She tossed the paper, an afternoon edition, on to the bed, and started pacing up and down the room.

> A popular cabaret dancer was brutally murdered last night in Amsterdam. The identity of the murderer is known, as he left some documents in the room where the crime took place. So far the indications are that the crime was motiveless, and the murderer a homicidal maniac.

Jeanne kept casting eager glances at Kees, expecting to see some sign of emotion. But there was none, and it was in a quite ordinary tone that he said to her:

'Would you mind handing me my coat?'

Naïvely she felt the pockets to make sure it wasn't a weapon he meant to take from it. It was only a cigar. He lit it with exasperating slowness, then, standing his pillow lengthways and propping his back against it, began reading the article, occasionally moving his lips:

> The latest information goes to show that Popinga left his home in Groningen under circumstances suggesting he may well be guilty of another murder. We learn that his employer, M. Julius de Coster, disappeared mysteriously on the previous night and . . .

'Well?' Jeanne's voice was shrill with impatience. 'That's you, isn't it?'

'Of course it is!'

'And you strangled that girl?'

'Well, I didn't intend to kill her. In fact, I can hardly understand how what I did could kill her. In any case, what the paper says is grossly exaggerated, and there are some downright lies.'

He got out of bed and headed for the bathroom.

'What are you up to?'

'Can't you see? I'm dressing. I'm going to have some lunch.'

'But it's five in the afternoon.'

'Well, dinner then.'

'What do you propose to do afterwards?'

'Haven't an idea.'

'Aren't you afraid of being arrested?'

'They'll have to recognize me first.'

'And where will you sleep? Don't you know you may be asked to show your identity papers?'

'Well, yes, that might be rather a nuisance.'

He hadn't yet had time to think things out, and his sleep had been so deep that it was an effort to collect himself.

'I'll give my mind to that presently,' he said. 'Do you know, I haven't even a toothbrush! Isn't it Christmas Eve today?'

'Yes.'

'Do you have Christmas trees and all that in this country on Christmas Day?'

'Yes, but it's Christmas Eve that really counts. Everybody makes a night of it in the restaurants and cafés, and of course one dances . . . Look here! You aren't trying to pull my leg by any chance?'

'Why should you think that?'

'I don't know . . . But I can't help wondering if you're not trying to make me think that you're Popinga, just for the fun of it.'

Again! How queer that people should always be wanting to foist on him a personality that wasn't his – to assume he couldn't be Kees Popinga!

'Anyhow,' Jeanne continued, 'there's something I want to tell you. I can't promise anything as yet, and I dare say I'm a damned fool to bother about it at all. But I shall be seeing someone this evening and I'll have a talk with him about you. Don't be alarmed, he has nothing to do with the police; it's a fellow who could give you a helping hand if he feels like it. Only, I don't know if he'll agree. That sort of crime –

strangling a girl just for the fun of it – well, it makes one think a bit.'

He went on lacing his black shoes as she talked.

'I shan't be seeing him till lateish. Know the Rue de Douai? No? It's quite near, anyone will tell you the way. There's a *tabac* there that stays open all night; just sit there and wait. I'll drop in just before midnight or perhaps a bit after – I can't say exactly, as there'll be a whole crowd of us on the binge tonight and it won't be too easy to get away.'

She gave him a final glance and picked up the newspaper from the bed.

'Wouldn't do to leave that lying about here. That's the way lots of fellows get copped. Wait a bit! I'll settle the hotel bill for you; that way they won't take so much notice of you on your way out. They're a bit surprised already at your sleeping so late. That's another sign, you know.'

'A sign of what?'

But she merely shrugged her shoulders and walked out, repeating:

'At the *tabac* in the Rue de Douai. Don't forget!'

Towards eight o'clock, when the Boulevards were growing crowded in anticipation of the night's festivities, Kees suddenly halted at a newspaper stall. On the front page of a late edition was a portrait with the caption: '*The Man Who Murdered Pamela* (wired from Amsterdam).'

He was flabbergasted. Where on earth had they unearthed this photograph? He had no recollection of it himself. However, on a closer inspection, he noticed the dim outline of another face near his, and understood. The person beside him was his wife. It came from the group photograph of himself and his family which stood on the sideboard. His portrait had been cut out and enlarged, and, still worse, disfigured, for it was all mottled as if it had been out in a shower of rain.

When at another kiosk the same picture confronted him, he felt almost annoyed at the poorness of the likeness. It might be the portrait of anyone – of any of the men passing in the street; it wasn't he at all!

> The murderer's wife believes her husband must suddenly have lost his memory . . .

At the next kiosk he bought a copy of the paper and asked to be shown the other evening editions. Four were pointed out to him and he bought them all.

'Have you any Dutch papers?'

'No, you can get them at the kiosk near the Opéra.'

The streets were a blaze of light, and posters at the entrances of restaurants were announcing Christmas Eve suppers at prices ranging from twenty-five to a hundred francs, all in. The night was still quite young, but there was a foretaste of gaiety in the air.

'I want all the Dutch newspapers you have,' Kees said.

His eyes fell on the Paris *Daily Mail*, and he was almost startled to see the photograph confronting him there as well.

'The *Daily Mail* too . . . Oh, and the *Morning Post*.'

The more papers he amassed, the more pleased he felt; it reminded him of old days; he had always enjoyed seeing the work piling up on his desk in the office.

How was the time going? Looking at his watch, he found he had some hours in hand before his appointment at the *tabac*, and decided to have some dinner. He entered the Café de la Paix, where the waiters were putting the finishing touches to the decorations, fixing up paper festoons and sprigs of mistletoe.

It reminded him that Amersen must have delivered at his house that morning the Christmas tree which he had ordered in advance. What would they do about it? And how was Frida feeling now? He had never given a thought to such side-issues when reading about crimes in the newspapers. But now that he himself was in the thick of it, so to speak, he couldn't help foreseeing all sorts of minor complications that would arise.

For instance, he had insured his life. What line does an insurance company take when a policy-holder is convicted of murder?

He had asked for a rare steak, and the waiter, as he placed it on the table, inquired:

'Is it as you like it, sir?'

'Couldn't be better!' he replied with gusto.

Unfortunately he was badly placed for reading the newspapers while he ate, and he had another disappointment when the sweet proved much less tasty than those provided in Dutch restaurants. Not sugared enough, for one thing. Also, he always had whipped cream and vanilla sugar with his coffee, and the waiter seemed quite disconcerted when he asked for them.

Anyhow, he had made an impression on Jeanne Rozier. Such an impression that she was taking him under her protection, though he had asked nothing of her. What sort of impression? he wondered. That of a cool customer, presumably. That indeed was how he saw himself. Just to prove it, he went up to a policeman at the corner of the Boulevard des Capucines and asked him the way to the Rue de Douai.

He found the *tabac* easily enough: a corner shop with a counter in front and a back room serving as a café, with eight tables. Kees went through into the café and was lucky enough to find a vacant table from which he could see, through a glass-panelled door, to the street outside. The neon lights in the cabarets across the road were beginning to light up, but their staff, including the professional dancers, were still exchanging confidences and having drinks at the bar, a few yards from Kees. In the corner facing him sat a flower-seller, a cup of coffee and a glass of rum on her table, her basket on the floor beside her chair.

'Waiter! I'll have a coffee too, please.'

He was rather depressed by this Parisian Christmas Eve which was getting under way around him; it wasn't like a real Christmas Eve – more like a rowdy wedding. By nine in the evening there were already plenty of drunks about – and he hadn't heard anyone speak of going to the midnight mass.

> (From our Special Correspondent in Groningen)
> While my colleague at Amsterdam is continuing his inquiry at the Carlton, where the unhappy cabaret dancer was done to death, I have been to Groningen to glean some information as to the antecedents of the murderer, Kees Popinga . . .

Kees sighed as he used to sigh when one of his subordinates at the office had made some particularly fatuous error, took out his notebook and, after entering the name and date of the newspaper, wrote: '*Not murderer, but involuntary author of her death. It should be borne in mind that the death was accidental.*'

He cast a glance at the flower-seller, who was having a nap till the theatre-goers began coming out, then went on reading:

> To my vast surprise I learn that Popinga enjoyed the high esteem of all who knew him, and that something like consternation prevails in Groningen at the discovery he is a criminal. Various hypotheses are mooted . . .

He underlined ironically the words 'hypotheses' and 'mooted', which he judged high-flown.

> At his home, where the grief of his family was most distressing to witness, Mrs Popinga was good enough to inform us . . .

Between two puffs of his cigar, composedly, he wrote in the notebook: '*So Mum deigned to let herself be interviewed by a journalist!*'

The Man Who Watched the Trains Go By

Then he smiled; the flower-seller's head had abruptly sagged forward over her chest.

> . . . to inform us that the only possible explanation of her husband's aberration is a sudden fit of madness, or loss of memory.

He amused himself by underlining the word 'aberration', all the quainter if Mum had actually used it.

Then, choosing a blank page of the notebook, he recorded: '*Mrs Popinga's "hypothesis": madness or loss of memory.*'

He learned that she wasn't the only one to hold such views. A young storekeeper at de Coster's, a lad of seventeen who, as it happened, owed his job to Kees, had the effrontery to say:

> I often used to notice a peculiar glitter in his eyes!

As for Dr Claes, he stated with calm assurance:

> The only possible explanation of Popinga's act is a sudden brainstorm. As his medical adviser, I am not at liberty to divulge whether any predispositions to insanity existed in his case.

So all agreed he was a madman. At least, until the suggestion was put forward that he might be responsible for Julius de Coster's death as well. On which assumption old Copenghem had pompously informed the journalist:

> Distasteful as it is to speak ill of a fellow-member of our Chess Club, I must own that no unprejudiced observer could fail to see that Popinga was an embittered man, who hated to admit that anyone excelled him in any field of activity, and was always nursing projects of revenge. If we assume that this inferiority complex had grown to an obsession with him, we can easily understand . . .

x

63

Popinga jotted down in his notebook: '*Copenghem: my "inferiority complex"!*'; and added in a smaller hand beneath it: '*He beat me only once at chess, and that by accident . . . Inferiority, indeed!!*'

By ten there was not an empty seat left in the café and he was being steadily edged off towards the end of the wall-sofa on which he was sitting. But he was almost unaware of this. Now and again he looked up from his newspapers and his notebook, gazed at a new arrival, frowned, then gave no more thought to those around him. Thus he did not notice that four or five Negroes had joined the company. The flower-seller was still there. People in evening-dress were wedged in between nondescripts in shabby, threadbare attire. He didn't realize that he was in the backstage of Montmartre, sitting with the bit-part players, while the celebrations were getting underway in all the local establishments

> A porter at Groningen station remembers noticing a man in a state of great excitement who . . .

Peevishly he wrote: '*What nonsense!*' Let them talk of brainstorms or an inferiority complex if they wanted, but really it was too absurd for words to declare that, because he was to kill Pamela – unintentionally – later in the day, he was in an excited state on leaving Groningen. Was he in an excited state now – even after drinking two cups of strong black coffee in quick succession?

And that porter at the Carlton, really he was the limit! The fellow deserved a good hiding!

> As soon as I saw the man I realized there was something odd about him, and I thought of warning Miss Mackinsen (Pamela). [Kees wrote: 'Then why didn't he do so?']
>
> When he came downstairs I was struck by his facial appearance; it was that of a wild beast at bay.' [' "Facial appearance" indeed! And has he ever seen a wild beast at bay?']

Thereupon he looked up and saw a young man in a dinner jacket staring hard at him. Behind the young man stood Jeanne, who said in a low tone:

'This is my friend Louis. I'll leave you men together.'

'Just come with me for a moment,' said Louis, his hands in his pockets, a cigarette dangling from his lips. 'Leave your things here. We'll step downstairs.'

He led Kees down to the lavatory, which was in the base-ment, and, after a good look at him, said in a low voice:

'Jeanne's told me all about it. And I've had a squint at the papers ... I must say you're a queer card! Do you often get taken that way?'

Popinga smiled. From the way in which the young man was looking at him, full in the eyes, with a glint of amusement, he guessed that Louis anyhow wouldn't start talking of insanity or inferiority complexes.

'No.' It was all he could do not to laugh. 'I'm not often taken that way. That was the first time.'

'What about the old cove – your boss?'

'Oh, they've got hold of the wrong end of the stick. De Coster was in a nasty jam – he'd been speculating – and did a bolt. Tried to make people think he'd drowned himself. As a matter of fact, that explains why ...'

'That can wait. I'm in a hurry. Know how to drive?'

'A car? Certainly.'

'It comes to this, if I've understood Jeanne rightly; what you need is somewhere to lie low till you can lay hands on some identity papers.'

He took the cigar from Popinga's lips and lit his cigarette with it. Then added nonchalantly:

'Well, we'll see about that later. You'd better wait here. There's a crowd of us going to have supper over the way.'

It was nearly midnight. The flower-seller had left; also some of the Negroes. Now and again a commissionaire from one of the cabarets would step across with a taxi-driver or some fur-tive night-bird for a quick one and a chat; then return to his post on the opposite pavement.

Never could Popinga have imagined so drab and ineffectual a Christmas Eve; even when a church clock struck midnight he waited in vain for the customary chime of bells. A drunkard staggered to his feet and bawled out the first line of a carol – all he knew of it apparently – and that was all. Even the owner of the café seemed to feel that something was lacking, for he went to the wireless set, and a moment later the air was reverberating with organ-notes and the voices of a male choir singing a Christmas anthem.

Kees folded up his newspapers and ordered another coffee, for he had lost his taste for alcohol. He followed the watch-night service coming through on the wireless and waited for the *Dominus vobiscum* as the priest turned towards the congregation.

There was a girl with extremely pale cheeks seated immedi-ately in front of him. Her pallor he attributed to the coldness of the night, for she came back to the café every hour or so looking more perished each time, after, presumably, having walked the streets in vain.

More and more cars were drawing up outside the cabarets. Three Negroes were engaged in heated argument – about what? Kees idly wondered. How strange to think that at this very moment, in every corner of the world, all the churches were filled with people singing, worshipping . . . ! For a moment he felt as if he were looking down on the world from a plane that had zoomed to a fantastic altitude; he saw it as a big snow-clad ball, studded with towns and villages, each of them nailed down to the earth by a tall, tapering church spire. And in every church were lights and incense, men and women gazing at a cradle . . .

No, that was nonsense! For one thing, midnight mass was

over in Central Europe, because it was already one o'clock there and in America at this hour it was still broad daylight. And there were plenty of people everywhere not in church; Negroes, for instance, exchanging dark confidences, and prostitutes sipping coffee with a dash of brandy in it to warm themselves up after walking the streets – not to mention hotel porters unburdening their hearts to Pressmen.

He had got over his sentimental mood. He no longer had any wish to hear the carol belched from the wireless; indeed, the owner of the café, who had imagined he would please his customers – or had he been a choirboy in his youth? – was obliged to switch it off, as everybody was grumbling at the noise.

Again the voices of the people in the room became audible. Clouds of cigarette smoke formed a blue canopy five feet under the white ceiling. A young man in a closely fitting dinner jacket had taken the seat facing Kees and was drinking mineral water, and now and again sniffing a pinch of white powder.

Why had he been asked if he could drive a car? And what would all these people round him say and do, were he to rise to his feet and announce point-blank: 'I'm Kees Popinga, the Amsterdam maniac!'?

At two in the morning he was still seated at the same place, and the waiter was beginning to treat him as an old acquaintance. At a loss what drink to order, he decided to follow the example of the youth facing him, and asked for mineral water. A few minutes later, when all the others sprang to their feet, he remained seated.

A quarrel had started at the bar, and people were shouting insults at each other. Someone flung a siphon, which burst on a table, and a moment later a struggling mass of people surged through the doorway into the street.

Somewhere a whistle shrilled. Quite composedly Kees picked up his newspapers, went downstairs to the lavatory and shut himself in one of the WCs, where he fell to reading the first article that caught his eye in one of his Dutch newspapers; it dealt with the economic development of Holland during the eighteenth century.

When he came upstairs a quarter of an hour later, all was calm and the broken glass on the floor had been swept up. But the room was empty. The waiter came up and greeted Kees with an understanding grin, for he had marked his customer's well-timed eclipse.

'Many people been arrested?' Kees asked.

'No, the cops aren't never very strict on Christmas Eve. They marched off two of them to the lock-up, but they'll let them out in the morning.'

Jeanne arrived in her evening dress, smelling of perfume, flushed and perspiring from her night's dancing. She had thrown a fur coat over her shoulders and had the air of having dropped round to see a neighbour.

'You've not had any trouble? Good! I was told you'd had a rough house over here.'

'Nothing to speak of.'

'I rather think Louis means to help you out. I can't get anything definite out of him – but he's always like that. Mind you don't go before I come back, anyhow ... You've no idea how hot it is over the way; there's such a crush you can hardly use your knife and fork.'

She seemed to have taken him under her wing, but at the same time kept eyeing him uneasily, as if he scared her a little.

'Not too bored hanging about like this?' she asked.

'Not in the least.'

Only after she had left did it strike him that her manner had changed; she had ceased to treat him as an ordinary 'pick-up' – and the change gratified him. She, anyhow, wasn't a soppy little fool like Pamela, who knew no better than to go into fits of witless laughter.

He took out the notebook and added to the page recording the views of Mum, the railwayman, Copenghem and some others: '*Anyhow, Mlle Rozier does not regard me as a lunatic.*'

A street-walker like the one who had been in and out of the café all the night accosted him and asked for a drink. He gave her five francs, making it clear she must expect no more from him.

He had folded his newspapers with care, and settled down to wait for Jeanne's return. Twice, for some reason, he recalled the strange expression of Frida's eyes and wondered what life had in store for her.

The room was stiflingly hot, but Kees had an impression that never before had his head been so cool, his brain so active. Would his wife carry out her plan of emigrating to Java and working in an hotel?

An idea crossed his mind of sending to the *Morning Post* a greeting for de Coster: just the words 'Good luck!'

There were no limits to his possibilities now that he had ceased playing the part of Kees Popinga, the model citizen, managing clerk of a well-established house. Incredible that, through all those years, he had sweated his soul out keeping up appearances, trying to perfect himself as a model of propriety! Still, that hadn't prevented Copenghem from telling the reporters . . .

Forthwith, if he felt like it, he could order a whole bottle of gin or brandy. Also if he'd felt like it he could have got off with that girl to whom he had just given five francs. He might even have asked that jumpy looking youngster for a pinch of cocaine. There was nothing to prevent him from – anything!

'Waiter, bring me another bottle of Perrier.'

It was a sort of protest against all these unbounded possibilities. Anyhow he had no desire for alcohol. He felt at the top of his form, drunk with his own lucidity! He was convinced that it would be the easiest thing in the world for him to make Jeanne fall in love with him and drop her gigolo.

Towards four in the morning she appeared again, slightly lit. She seemed impressed by finding him still there.

'Well, I must say you're a sticker!' Then went on, in a different tone: 'Louis and his friends are fighting shy a bit. But I did my best. This is what I've managed to fix up – it's the most they'd agree to. They'll be leaving the cabaret in a few minutes and they'll take two cars and drive straight to the Porte d'Italie. Know where that is?'

'No.'

'That's just too bad. In that case, you haven't a dog's chance, I'm afraid. They want you to take a car too. They'll wait for a few moments at the Porte d'Italie, and, when you get there, you're to blink your headlights as a signal. After that, you've only got to follow them.'

'Just a moment. Is the Porte d'Italie to the right or to the left?'

'Neither. You have to drive right across Paris.'

'I'll manage it. I'll ask the cops the way.'

'You're crazy – or you haven't tumbled to it. You're to *take* a car, one of the cars belonging to the people in the cabarets across the road.'

'I knew you meant that. And that's just why I'll ask the police – to inspire confidence, you see.'

'Well, I hope it works! Look here! I warn you Louis and his pals won't wait long. Oh, and there's another thing. Don't take a posh car. Choose one of the ordinary makes.'

She was sitting at his side, looking very pretty in her closely fitting evening-frock; for a moment he felt sorry he had let the opportunity slip by that night at the hotel. Silly of him not to notice she was so desirable . . .

'When shall I see you again?' he asked gently.

'Can't say. It'll depend on Louis . . . Hello! There they are, going out.'

He paid for the drinks and put on the grey overcoat, rolling up the papers to get them into the pocket. Two of the long line of cars drawn up beside the pavement moved away almost simultaneously.

'Well, won't you say *au revoir* to me?'

'Rather! I like you, Jeanne – very much indeed. You're one of the best!'

As soon as he was in the street, conscious that she was watching him from the window, he walked briskly along the line of cars, stepped into the fourth in the row, and pressed the starter home.

The car drew out from the pavement, followed for some yards a big saloon in which several women could be seen, and, when he turned to wave his hand to Jeanne, the *café-tabac* in the Rue de Douai in which he had spent this curious Christmas Eve was already out of sight.

5

*How Kees was properly revolted by the sight of a Popinga
in a sweater and dungarees cooped up in a garage, and
how once again he proved his independence*

It was almost ten in the morning, but the concierge was still
in her bed. The Christmas mail of the occupants of the building
was stacked up in a corner of her room, beside a sealed milk-
bottle and two long French rolls. The streets had the forlorn
air that streets always have on the morrow of a holiday; even
the taxis hadn't put in an appearance at their ranks, and nobody
was about except a few stalwart church-goers, their noses blue
with cold.

'Who's that?' Jeanne asked sleepily. For some minutes she
had been hearing a distant banging, but hadn't connected it
with the door of her flat.

'Police!'

The word jerked her awake. Feeling with her toes for the
slippers on the rug, she called in a rather peevish tone:

'Just a moment!'

She had slept by herself, for a change, in her flat in the Rue
Fromentin. The green silk dress sprawled across a chair, her
stockings were lying on the counterpane. She had kept on her
chemise, and now she flung a dressing-gown over it as she
walked to the door.

'What do you want?'

She knew the inspector by sight. He entered the bedroom,
took off his hat, and switched on the light, but all he had to
say was:

'Superintendent Lucas wants you to come to his office. He's sent me to fetch you.'

'So he works on holidays too, confound him!'

If anything, Jeanne looked even more attractive just hauled out of bed, with her auburn hair tumbling over her cheeks. But in the greenish eyes there was a glint of almost feline wariness. She went on with her dressing without troubling about the presence of the inspector, who kept his eyes fixed on her as he smoked a cigarette.

'What's it like outside?' she asked.

'Freezing.'

She applied some cursory make-up. When they were in the street she asked:

'Haven't you a taxi?'

'No, I was given no orders about it.'

'Then I'll pay for one. I've no wish to travel by bus halfway across Paris.'

When they reached the headquarters of the Police Judiciaire on the Quai des Orfèvres, where most of the staff were absent, she had, though one would never have guessed it from her expression, been thinking hard. She had reviewed every possible theory to account for this summons and had answers pat for almost every question the superintendent might ask her.

He made her wait a good quarter of an hour in the corridor, but Jeanne was too well used to the ways of the establishment to show the least impatience.

'Come in, my dear. Sorry to have made you get up at such an unholy hour.'

She seated herself beside the mahogany desk, planted her bag on it, and fixed her eyes on the bald, fatherly-looking superintendent.

'It's quite a while since we last saw you here, isn't it?' he remarked. 'If I remember rightly, the last time was three years ago, in connection with a dope case. By the way, I hear you've broken with Louis . . .'

The first two phrases had been mere by-play, to create an 'atmosphere'; the third made Jeanne start, and ask impulsively:

'Who . . . who told you that?'

'Afraid I can't remember. But last night, when I was in Montmartre, seeing Christmas in, someone told me you'd been getting very thick with some foreigner, an Englishman or a German.'

'That's a good one!' she laughed.

'Anyhow, that's why I asked you to come and look me up. I'd be sorry if you got into trouble.'

To hear them talk, one would have thought them old and trusted friends. The superintendent was pacing up and down the room, his thumbs stuck in the armholes of his waistcoat. He had offered a cigarette to his visitor and she was smoking it, her legs crossed above the knees, her eyes fixed on the scene outside the window – the grey bank of the Seine and a portion of a bridge over which buses rumbled now and again.

After pondering for some moments, she said:

'I rather think I know what you're driving at. It's that fellow I got off with the day before yesterday, you want to know about, isn't it?'

'Oh, so it was a pick-up, was it? From what I was told . . .' He paused.

'That's all there was to tell you, anyhow. I suppose it was Freddie, the head waiter at Picratts, who spoke to you about it. It was just on closing time when that Dutchman blew in, and he seemed set on making a night of it. He asked me to his table, ordered champagne and, just before we left, he changed some florins. After that we went to the Rue Victor-Massé; I always go to that hotel because it's nice and clean. We went to bed. He didn't even touch me . . .'

'Why?'

'How would I know? Anyhow, I was fed up sleeping with a fat lump of a Dutchman who took no notice of me, and I cleared off first thing in the morning.'

'With his money?'

'No. I woke him, and he gave me a thousand-franc note.'

'For doing . . . damn-all?'

'Well, that wasn't my fault.'

'Then you went home. Louis was there, I suppose?'

She nodded.

'By the way, where's Louis to be found just now? Is it a fact he wasn't at your place this morning?'

A flash of something like anger lit Jeanne's eyes, and she snarled:

'That's just what I'd like to know – where he is, the dirty sod!'

'Ah, so last night, too, you weren't with him?'

'No. We'd had quite a good time, there were a whole lot of us making a night of it. Some tart or other must have made a pass at him, for he sneaked off without letting me know, and he hasn't shown up since.'

'Does he do much work nowadays?'

She gave a harsh laugh.

'Why should he work? If he was making money on his own, why would he need me?'

Superintendent Lucas smiled discreetly. Jeanne made a slight movement, as though supposing the interview was over. They had played their respective parts to the best of their ability, and each remained on the defensive, keeping something back.

'Well, can I go back to bed?'

'Oh, certainly. But there's just one thing. If by any chance you come across that Dutchman of yours again –'

'I'll give the fellow a smack in the jaw! I've no use for that sort of swine who gets a kick out of murdering girls . . . Oh,

I know quite well why you've been grilling me for the last quarter of an hour. I've seen the papers. And, when I think I might have been done in like that poor girl in Amsterdam – well, it gives me the creeps!'

'Did you recognize him by the photo?'

'Well, no, I couldn't say that. It's not much like him. But, all the same, I guessed it was him all right.'

'What did he tell you? Did he say anything about his plans?'

'He asked me if I knew the South of France. I think he said something about Nice.'

She had risen to her feet. The superintendent thanked her politely, and a quarter of an hour later Jeanne was back in her flat. But, instead of going back to bed, she had a bath and got into one of her plainest dresses.

It was about half past twelve when she entered Chez Mélie, a small restaurant patronized by frequenters of the Rue Blanche. She had no appetite and ordered merely a glass of port.

'Louis?' asked the waiter, as if the name were a whole phrase in itself.

'Can't say. But I think he'll be coming.'

At three, however, he hadn't yet turned up. Leaving a message for him, Jeanne went to the nearest cinema. Not until five did somebody tap her lightly on the shoulder. Louis, at last.

'You're late,' she whispered.

'I had to go all the way to Poitiers.'

'Listen, Louis. We must have a talk. But not here. There may be someone listening behind us.'

They made their way to a crowded *brasserie* in the Rue Blanche and found a corner table.

'I was hauled out of bed this morning to go to the Quai des Orfèvres. Lucas, you know. That fellow who always talks to you as if you were his own daughter, but who is the biggest swine of the whole bunch. Where did you park that idiot Dutchman?'

'At Goin's. He's a cool customer, your Dutchman! Fernand, who was in the front car with me, bet he'd never get as far as the Porte d'Italie. Well, we'd hardly got there ourselves when we saw a car blinking its lights at us. We put our foot down to Juvisy. When we turned into the garage he was just behind us. You'd think he'd been on the game all his life!'

'What did he say?'

'Nothing! Goin was waiting for us with his mechanic. We all got down to the job and had it done within the hour. Rose made us some coffee. We got away before daylight with the three buses – except your Dutchman, who's to stay at Goin's till I find a way of making him cough up the money he certainly has, stowed away somewhere.'

'Better act cautious, though. The cops know I spent a night with him. If Lucas sent for me at ten o'clock on Christmas morning it means he's on to something.'

'Is he, the swine? Look here, I'd better ring up Goin and tell him right away.'

'I wouldn't say it over the 'phone. You never know who's listening in.'

For the other customers at the *brasserie*, they were just a young, well-dressed couple engaged in a tête-à-tête. Their faces betrayed nothing of their feelings.

'Anyhow, there's no urgent hurry,' said Jeanne in the tone of someone who has had enough of a subject. 'I'll have thought up something by tomorrow, and I'll give you the word. Tonight you'd better go somewhere where lots of people will see you – the boxing-match, or the cycle-race – please yourself.'

'Right-o! Do we dine together?'

'No. I said you were doing the dirty on me with another girl. You'd better dig one up and have her in tow.' As she spoke she was looking away from him. Suddenly she squeezed his thigh and added, 'But don't touch – or you'll be sorry for it!'

*

Why should Kees have been surprised, considering the revelations made by de Coster at the Saint George, and his present certitude that all he had believed in hitherto was so much moonshine? In former days he'd never have noticed that this garage had several queer features. Now, however, it struck him at once that a real garage isn't built a hundred yards back from the main road, up a blind alley, with two unlighted petrol pumps and doors that open of their own accord when one sounds one's horn in a special way.

He had also noticed that on an empty plot of land beside the garage were at least a dozen dismantled cars, relatively new ones. Most of them seemed to have been damaged in accidents and one was half burnt out. He had had time to read by the light of the headlights the notice over the entrance: '*Goin and Buret. Cars Repaired. Electrical Experts.*'

Finally he had watched, smoking a cigar, the activities that had followed their arrival. Two men were standing in the doorway: Goin, a burly middle-aged man, and a youngster whom everyone called Kiki. Goin was in brown overalls with spanners protruding from the pockets. He merely touched Louis's hand before settling down to work. Obviously he was an old hand at the job to which he now applied himself.

The second car had been driven by an amiable young fellow whose name Kees did not catch and who, like Louis and Fernand, was wearing a dinner jacket.

But for a light lorry and some tools the garage was empty. The walls were whitewashed, there was a big iron stove in a corner, and two powerful electric lamps cast a harsh light on the bare walls and floor of beaten earth.

When the others set to work, Louis took a suitcase from the light lorry, undressed, and, as calmly as an actor changing his costume behind a strip of scenery, got into a brown suit, knotted a yellow tie, then donned overalls and gave the others a hand.

Fernand and the pleasant-looking young man followed suit, while Goin manipulated an acetylene blowpipe and Kiki unscrewed the numberplates.

'Isn't Rose in?' asked Louis.

'She'll be here in a minute. I rang when I heard you coming.'

Kees noticed an electric bell-push beside a door at the far end of the shed, beyond which evidently were the living-quarters. And presently a youngish woman entered by it, scant-ily attired and still half asleep, and greeted them all like old friends – including Kees, whom, however, she eyed with some surprise.

'Only three buses!' she said scornfully. 'Not much for a night's work! But, of course, it's Christmas.'

'Hurry up and make some coffee for us . . . You'll have a snack, Louis, won't you?'

'No, thanks, I'm full to the neck with turkey.'

No one troubled to keep watch outside; evidently they felt quite safe here. Between two turns of a spanner they exchanged jokes and scraps of information.

'How's Jeanne?'

'Quite OK. It was she picked up our friend here – I want you to look after him till further notice. Keep your eyes peeled! He's in it up to the neck, and, if the cops get him . . .'

Within an hour all the numberplates had been changed; also the numbers of the chassis and engines. There was a kitchen behind the garage – quite a clean one, considering – and here Rose dispensed coffee, bread and butter and cold sausage.

'You,' said Louis to Kees as he sipped the scalding-hot coffee, 'you've got to lie low here, and do exactly what Goin tells you. Until you have identity papers no larking about for you, old boy! Next week we'll see about shifting you from here. Got it?'

'Yes,' said Kees cheerfully, 'I've got it!'

'Better be moving, hadn't we, the rest of us? Fernand will

take the Rheims road. You – you'd better skirt round Paris and try to sell the bus at Rouen. I'm off to Orléans. See you all this evening, boys. Bye-bye, Rose, my pet.'

At first Kees found it rather amusing to be plunged into these novel surroundings, rubbing shoulders with these people he didn't know. After locking up the garage, Goin, who was six-foot tall and even burlier than the skipper of *Ocean III*, dawdled over his second cup of coffee, rolling a cigarette, while Rose, her elbows planted on the table, stared dreamily into the middle distance.

'Foreigner, aren't you?'

'Dutch.'

'Then it would be safer to say you're English. We've a few Englishmen round about here. Know the lingo? Yes? That's good. Have the cops your description?'

While Kees, too, was having a second cup of coffee, with plenty of milk in it, Goin went upstairs and came back with a pair of shabby blue trousers, overalls like those he was wearing, and a thick grey sweater.

'Here, put these on! They should fit you. Rose will fix you up a bed in the dressing-room. The more sleep you put in while you're here the better, I should say.'

Rose went upstairs to get his bed ready. Goin, who kept dropping off to sleep, half closed his eyes and remained quite still, his legs stretched out in front of him. A voice came from the upper floor:

'It's ready.'

Goin rose heavily to his feet.

'She's fixed your bed. You'd better go up now. Good night.'

The staircase was dark and narrow. To get to the room assigned him, Kees had to make his way across the bedroom shared by Goin and Rose. The dressing-room was much smaller than the bedroom and contained only a camp-bed, a table, and a broken mirror hung on the wall.

'When you want to wash, there's a tap in the passage,' Rose told him. 'Hope you don't mind noise; we're just alongside the marshalling-yard and you'll hear trains shunting and whistling at all hours.'

After she had closed the door, he pressed his face to the window-pane and saw in the dim light a wilderness of railway lines, strings of carriages, whole trains, and a dozen or so locomotives spurting vivid white plumes of steam against the greyness of the daybreak.

He smiled, stretched himself, and sat down on the bed. A quarter of an hour later he was sleeping profoundly, fully dressed.

He was still asleep when Jeanne was summoned to the Superintendent's office. And still asleep when she ordered a port at the restaurant in the Rue Blanche, and also when, towards two, Rose peeped in at the door, surprised not to have heard him moving.

He did not rise till three, then put on the new clothes – they made him look much stouter – and tiptoed down the stairs. In the kitchen he found a place laid at the end of the table.

'Do you like rabbit?'

'Very much.'

There was nothing eatable he didn't like!

'Where's your husband?' he asked.

'Oh, he's not my husband. He's my brother. He's gone to a football match ten miles from here.'

'Haven't the others come back?'

'They never call back here.'

'How about Jeanne – Jeanne Rozier? Does she drop in sometimes?'

'Why on earth should she? She's the boss's woman.'

Though he couldn't have said why, he had a great desire to see Jeanne again. How annoying to be cut off from her like this! He could think of nothing else while he ate his rabbit, dipping his bread in the rich brown gravy.

'I suppose I can take a stroll, can't I?'

'Charles didn't say so.'

'Who's Charles?'

'My brother. Goin, if you prefer.'

A queer young woman; at first sight you might take her for a maid-of-all-work in her Sunday best! Her face was pale, almost cadaverous; she put too much red on her lips and wore a flame-coloured silk dress that didn't suit her, and absurdly high-heeled shoes.

'Will you stay at the garage all the afternoon?'

'Somebody's got to mind it. But this evening I'm going out dancing.'

He decided to have a stroll. All the people in the streets were in their Sunday clothes in honour of Christmas Day. Clad in the sweater and the shabby trousers, he strolled about, his hands in his pockets. On a sudden impulse he turned into a shop to buy a pipe; they had a poor selection, but he bought one all the same, filled it, and entered a café where he had noticed people playing Russian pool.

In one corner he discovered a complicated slot-machine of the gambling type. When a franc was inserted, wheels began to spin and came to rest in various combinations of fruit, according to which one could win sums ranging from two to sixteen francs, or even all the money in the pot.

Kees handed the barman a fifty-franc note, saying:

'Give me the change in francs, please.'

Half an hour later he asked for another fifty; the game had caught his fancy. By this time, everybody was watching him; some had come quite close to watch the *coups*. He had taken the red notebook from his pocket and was recording the scores methodically.

By five the air was thick with cigarette smoke, and he was

still at it, taking no notice of what went on around him, for he was beginning to understand.

'It comes to this,' he said to the proprietor of the café, who was standing near him. 'One coin in two falls into a special compartment reserved for the owner of the machine. A fifty per cent rake-off, in fact.'

'I don't know anything about that. It isn't our machine. The people who brought it here come to collect the takings.'

'How often do they come?'

'Once a week or so. That depends.'

'And how much do they get out of the machine?'

'Haven't a notion.'

Grins were exchanged when they saw him making complicated calculations, then starting to play again. Not a muscle of his face stirred when eight or twelve francs rattled down into the drawer marked 'Winnings'. He merely pocketed them, jotted down a figure, and put another franc into the slot.

Those present were mostly railwaymen and, without stopping playing, Kees asked one of them:

'Is it a big station here?'

'It's the biggest goods-station in Paris. All the marshalling is done here . . . Excuse my saying so, but that's a mug's game you're at! The longer you play, the more you lose.'

'I know.'

'Then why do you go on playing?'

He had given up smoking the pipe, which incommoded him, and bought cigars. He had a short drink, the name of which he didn't know; but he'd noticed that most of the others were drinking it and the colour had taken his fancy.

What a fantastic Christmas Day! No one seemed to dream of going to church, not a bell was pealing! At one table they were playing cards. There was a whole family: father, mother, and two kids. The man was playing with his friends while the others watched, the children occasionally taking sips from their father's glass.

Kees had finished his calculations. Pleased with himself, he walked to the bar and again addressed the proprietor.

'Do you know how much a machine like that brings in. At least a hundred francs a day. Now suppose it cost five thousand francs . . .'

A man beside him interrupted:

'But what if somebody hits the jackpot?'

'That makes no difference. Listen! I'll explain . . .'

Two pages of his notebook were covered with equations. They listened, but his explanation was beyond them. As he went out, someone asked:

'Who is he?'

'Haven't an idea. A foreigner, I should say.'

'Where does he work?'

'I don't know that either. He's left two hundred francs in that machine. Rum customer, isn't he?'

'A bit barmy, I should say.'

A railwayman remarked sagely:

'Foreigners always seem barmy. I reckon it's because we don't understand 'em.'

Goin returned from the football match and Rose went out to dance. After closing the garage, Goin got into carpet slippers, rolled a cigarette and settled down to reading the evening paper in the kitchen. He looked the picture of well-fed content. Meanwhile Kees was jotting down some notes:

> *Profit on the three cars – 30,000 francs at lowest estimate. Assuming a similar haul each week – an easy matter – the profit for a year would be . . .*

And added underneath:

Wish I could see Jeanne again and discover why she sent me here.

Thereupon he went upstairs and, before getting into bed, gazed for several minutes at the glimmering expanse of railway lines, red and green lights, a long, black goods train rumbling by. His thoughts kept harking back to Jeanne, and now he found a curious pleasure in picturing amorous contacts which, when they were available, he had forgone.

When he rose at ten next morning there was a thin coat of snow, not on the road (where it had melted), but between the rails and on the embankments. He found Rose in the kitchen and asked where her brother was.

'He's gone to Paris.'

In the garage was nobody except Kiki, who was sticking out his tongue, like a schoolboy wrestling with a hard sum, as he adjusted a magneto.

'I'd like to go to Paris too,' he remarked to Rose.

'My brother told me not to let you. You've only got to read the morning paper, so he said.'

'What's in it?'

'Dunno. I haven't looked.'

Strange girl – to feel so little curiosity! She went on browning onions in a pan and didn't even look round when Kees unfolded the newspaper.

> In view of the difficulties with which the police have to contend we must be guarded in our statements as to the latest developments in this case. Meanwhile, however, we are authorized to state that Christmas was not a holiday for everyone and that Superintendent Lucas of the Police Judiciaire has put in some very useful work on it. The arrest of the homicidal maniac from Amsterdam may be expected at any moment.

Really, those journalists! Angrily Kees underscored the word 'maniac', and with an acid smile stared at Rose's back, observing that the morning wrap she was wearing made her look still broader in the beam than usual.

> The latest news from Holland indicates that sensational developments may be expected, as Julius de Coster's business has just gone into liquidation, and it appears that Popinga had invested all his savings in the firm. May not de Coster's disappearance be due to an act of vengeance on Popinga's part?

And so on.

Of what he had read, only a name stuck in his memory: 'Superintendent Lucas.' Then he went to the stove, lifted the lid of a saucepan and peeped underneath. The rest of the morning he spent at the little café, empty at this hour, gambling at the slot-machine and chatting with the proprietor.

When he returned to the garage he found Goin back, but dressed so elegantly as to be hardly recognizable.

'Ah, so you're here at last!' Goin exclaimed irritably. 'Going off your knocker, aren't you? Where the hell have you been?'

'In a little café I've taken a fancy to.'

'Well, let me tell you the latest. I saw the boss this morning. Yesterday an inspector came and yanked Jeanne out of bed and took her to the Quai des Orfèvres. Know what that means? It looks as if we'll have a deal of trouble before we're finished with you.'

'What did she say?'

'Who?'

'Mademoiselle Rozier.'

'I didn't see her. Anyhow, the boss says you're to keep in your bedroom and not to show your ruddy nose outside. Got it? Rose will bring your meals. For the next few days, until Louis gives the word, you got to lie low here.'

'Not eating anything?' Rose inquired.

'Thanks, I'm waiting for my helping.'

'When he dumped you on us, I'd no notion it was anything so serious. I say, why on earth did you do it? Are you really nuts?'

'I don't understand that word.'

'I mean, do you often get taken like that, wanting to strangle women?'

'It was the first time. And, if she hadn't laughed . . .'

He began eating the stewed beef and chips to which Rose had helped him.

'Listen!' said Goin grimly. 'Get this into your thick head. If you lay a finger on my sister I'll wring your bloody neck. If I'd known the sort of customer you were . . .'

Kees thought quickly. No, it wasn't worth answering the man; he'd never understand. The best thing was to go on quietly with his meal.

'Once you're back in your bedroom, you'll damned well stay there. Got it? It was quite bad enough your gadding about in the cafés in Juvisy. You didn't talk to anyone, by any chance?'

'I did.'

The funniest thing was that it should be Goin who was getting worked up, whereas Kees remained calm and was eating heartily.

'Shouldn't be surprised if one of these days the boss finds he's made a big mistake about you. I was fooled myself; I took you for somebody worth helping out – blast you!'

The man was in a towering rage. Meanwhile Rose, as she went on with her meal, kept her eye on the range, like a good housewife, while Kiki sat, eating, on the doorstep, his plate on his knees.

Kees preferred not to say what he thought. He gave the impression of taking it lying down – which encouraged Goin to continue:

'The boss'll be back in three days anyhow. He's got to be in Marseilles tonight, but the moment he's back . . .'

Kees had decided how to behave. He ate the last mouthful, wiped his lips with his handkerchief, and rose from his chair.

'I'm going upstairs. Good afternoon.'

They didn't return his 'Good afternoon', or make any comment on his departure. When he was on the landing, Goin shouted after him reluctantly:

'If you need anything, you've only got to stamp on the floor three times. The kitchen's just below your room, and Rose will hear.'

Kees wasn't feeling sleepy. He went to the little window and, resting his elbows on the sill, let his gaze roam the landscape: a fantastic landscape with a background of snow-clad fields, and near at hand rows of grimy sheds, iron girders, all the monstrous paraphernalia of a big goods station – trucks moving by themselves, unattached engines marking time, snorting and whistling impatiently, and a few sad trees, survivors of a rural age, fretting the wintry sky with a tangle of bare branches.

Of all that had been told him Kees bore in mind only one fact: that Louis had left, or was about to leave, for Marseilles.

Towards four, seated on his bed under the shadeless electric bulb, he read again:

> The superintendent has questioned a young woman, Jeanne R—, of 13 Rue Fromentin, and she ...

It was cold, and Kees had wrapped the cotton blanket round him and drawn the camp-bed near the kitchen stove pipe which ran through his room on its way roofwards. Trains were whistling incessantly, and all the sounds outside merged in a counter-point of stridences: shrill notes and deep ones, the rhythmic panting of engines, clangs of dark iron, and now and again the drone of a car speeding along the main road.

So Louis was off to Marseilles. And, here, this sallow-faced girl, Rose, didn't even trouble to read the paper and find out who he was! Louis was definitely hostile, raging inwardly against him. Likely as not already selling him to the police.

Still, what did it matter? He could always shrug his shoulders and gaze derisively at the rough sweater and the overalls that travestied for a while the real Popinga. He was in a stronger position than any of them, even Louis, even Jeanne. For the whole gang was, so to speak, tied to the garage, much as Mum was tied to her house, Dr Claes to his practice and to Eleanore, Copenghem to the chess club, whose presidency he coveted.

They were all tied, whereas he, Popinga, was tied to nothing, to no one, to no set idea – and he would prove it to them very soon.

6

*Of the indiscretions of a
stove pipe and Kees Popinga's
second crime*

He might easily have dozed off in the warmth from the stove pipe, through which he could, so to speak, feel the flames burning, had he not distinctly heard the kitchen door open and someone walk up to the range, and then a noise which drowned all other sounds – of someone poking the fire. As the racket subsided he heard Goin ask:

'Did you listen at the door? What's he up to?'

Rose answered grumpily:

'I don't know. I haven't heard him move once.'

'Will you make me a cup of coffee?'

'All right . . . What are you messing about with there?'

'Can't you see? I'm trying to fix up the blasted alarm clock. It conked out this morning.'

Kees grinned. He could picture the two of them in the room below: Goin in slippers, a dead cigarette stuck to his under-lip, knitting his brows as he took down, or assembled, the alarm clock on the kitchen table, while his sister – judging by the sounds – washed up.

'Say, Rose, what's your idea of that Dutchman?'

The voices sounded all the more muffled as the two below exchanged the odd remark by way of idle chit-chat. There were long pauses, and sometimes the rumble of a passing train drowned what they were saying. Pleasantly conscious of the waves of heat flooding the little room, Kees closed his eyes and listened.

'My idea? Well, there's something queer about him; I wouldn't trust that man, not one inch! What's he done?'

'I've only just heard. It seems he strangled a cabaret dancer in Amsterdam, and may have plugged an old boy, too, the day before.'

For all his lethargy, Kees fished out his notebook and jotted down the word 'plug'.

A kettle started singing below; Rose ground some coffee; a cup and sugar-bowl chinked on the wooden table.

'Wish I could work out where this cog goes . . .'

'Did you meet Louis?'

'Yes. And I asked him what he proposed to do about our friend upstairs.'

'What did he say?'

'Oh, you know how he is. He likes pretending he's a deep one and plans things out beforehand. But, if you ask me, I don't believe he knows what he's doing half the time; he just barges ahead and trusts to luck. He tried to make me think he has this fellow in his pocket and can make him cough up any amount. That's all very fine and large, but, as I told him, that fellow has *us* in his pocket, in a manner of speaking . . .'

'Drink your coffee while it's hot . . . Look! There's a screw you've dropped just beside your chair.'

'When you say anything to Louis he gets his rag out and starts telling you that it's his responsibility and you've only got to let him get on with it. But I tell him: "For the cars, OK, boss. But I don't much care about having a fellow like that Dutchie at my place. I got my sister to think about." '

'Oh, I'm not afraid of him.'

'Not to mention that it might easily land us in clink. My idea is that it's Jeanne who badgered Louis into taking up with this fellow. Louis hadn't the spunk to say "No" to her, and so he said "Yes" without thinking it through. Great! Let's see what happens next . . .'

Sounds travelled up the stove pipe so clearly that Kees seemed to see Goin winding up the alarm clock, which at last he had assembled.

'Got it right?'

The only answer was a metallic clash; in an access of rage, the man had hurled the clock across the kitchen. After a while he said:

'Buy another one tomorrow morning. Hasn't the paper-boy been round yet?'

'No.'

'Anyhow, I gave Louis a straight tip. Now that a chance has come our way we'd better put ourselves in good with the cops by handing over this damned "maniac" as they call him. It might make things easier for us if ever they start snoopin' round the garage.'

'What did he say to that?'

'Nothing. He'll see about it when he's back from Marseilles.'

'Have they the guillotine in Holland?'

'Dunno. Why do you want to know?'

There was a short silence; then Goin added rather uncomfortably:

'Of course, if he was an ordinary sort of bloke I wouldn't have talked like that. But you see what I mean, Rose, don't you? You got to consider the sort of things he does. Wait! I'll go and buy a paper; then you'll understand.'

Kees hadn't stirred. The room was in darkness but for a faint glow coming through the window from the lights hung in midair above the marshalling-yard. He could hear Rose padding about below in her felt slippers, opening cupboards, placing crockery on a shelf, then shooting a shovelful of coals into the range.

The time passed slowly. Goin's talk of going to buy a paper had been no doubt a pretext for visiting the local, where probably he had settled down to a game of cards. He did not return till two hours later, when the table was laid for dinner.

'Nobody come?'

'No.'

'What about the chap upstairs?'

'I haven't heard a sound. He's asleep, I expect.'

'Do you know what I was thinking on the way back? That a man like that's a bigger threat to society than we are. I know that Louis once got busy with his gun – but that was because he was in a tight corner. At least, with folks like us you know where you are. But that fellow upstairs . . . ! Can you imagine, Rose, what he's thinking now?'

'Anyhow, he must be feeling pretty low,' Rose sighed.

'Well, whose fault is that? Anyhow, as I said just now, I don't want none of his sort under my roof . . . Hell! Rabbit again! Is it on special offer, or something?'

'There was some left over from yesterday.'

'You'll have to take him up his grub.'

'I'll go up presently.'

A few minutes later Rose knocked at Kees's door saying:

'Let me in. I've brought your dinner.'

Kees was on his feet. The door remained open and he deliberately planted himself between her and the doorway, screwing up his eyes and staring at her with ominous intentness.

'You, anyhow, are a good sort,' he remarked. Perhaps he hardly knew as yet whether he wanted to frighten her a little, or had some more serious design. 'Now that you've come in you'll stay a moment, won't you?'

She swung round, examined him from head to foot without a trace of nervousness.

Then, 'Aw, cut it out!' she said roughly, watching his eyes, his awkward smile and twitching hands. 'You don't take me for a cabaret tart by any chance, do you? . . . The best thing you can do is to eat your dinner and go to bed.'

Coolly, by sheer presence of mind, she compelled him to make way for her. As she went out she said:

'When you've finished, put the tray outside.'

A moment later Kees had his ear an inch or so from the stove pipe, and presently he heard the door of the kitchen open and close. A chair scraped on the floor; Rose was sitting down. A wine glass chinked against a bottle.

'Was he asleep?'

'I suppose so.'

'Did he say anything?'

'Why should he say anything?'

'Oh, I thought I heard you talking together.'

'I told him to have his grub and put the tray outside.'

'Don't you agree with me that Louis is acting foolish? If Lucas sent for Jeanne he must be on to something. I'll bet Jeanne is being watched, and Louis too. Shouldn't be a bit surprised if the cops spotted me talking to him today. For all I know, they may have shadowed me here . . .'

'So you want to turn him in?'

'Well, if it wasn't for Louis . . .'

He evidently buried himself in his newspaper, for there followed a long silence. At last he yawned and said:

'How about turning in? There'll be nothing doing tonight. I'll lock up the garage.'

Kees did as Rose had told him and placed the tray outside. After that he closed the door securely. Then he took off the clothes that Goin had lent him and got into his grey suit, replacing in its pockets what money remained to him, and the notebook.

There was no hurry. He lay on the bed, the blanket drawn over him, and waited, listening to the sounds in the next room, as Goin and his sister got undressed, exchanged the odd word, clattered around a bit then got into bed. Probably, he reflected, they had spent their childhood in some tenement where it was the normal thing for families to sleep five or six in the same room.

After a while he heard a sleepy voice say, ' 'night, Rose,' and hers reply, ' 'night.' Then the man's voice came again.

'I'm not saying I know everything, and I can tell you don't feel the same as me. But one day we'll see who's right.'

'Yes, we'll see,' she echoed, acquiescent or, more likely, half asleep already.

Kees waited for a quarter of an hour, half an hour, then slipped off the bed and tiptoed to the window. Snow was falling again. He had a moment's hesitation; once the window was open, the din from the goods yard would pour in, and mightn't it wake the sleepers in the next room?

Anyhow, it would all be over so quickly, that would hardly matter. Immediately below the window was a lorry with a tarpaulin roof; it was little more than a five-foot drop. Kees climbed out, hung by his hands for a moment, then let himself fall. Two seconds later he was walking briskly across the patch of waste land behind the garage, leaving footprints in the thin layer of snow.

He wanted to know the time, and found his watch was gone from his pocket; probably Goin had filched it. After taking his bearings he walked to Juvisy. As he was passing the little café where the slot-machine was, he all but entered, just to show how he looked in ordinary life, with a collar and tie and a well-cut overcoat.

The station clock told him the time: twenty to eleven. He went to the booking-office and asked the clerk in a polite tone when was the next train to Paris.

'In twelve minutes.'

Waiting on the platform, he had a very real feeling of escape.

Not that the idea of being in danger had worried him at any moment, but he had had a sensation, unknown to him since his departure from Groningen, of being caged; it was as if in coming to this suburban hideout he had suddenly lost all that his escape had given him.

Almost it seemed as if he were under the wing of others again – with Louis, Goin, and Rose replacing his wife, the family, and office! Really, these Parisians had understood him no better than had the worthy folk of his home town.

What was that odd word Goin had used? He looked it up in his notebook. 'Plugged.' Yes, they actually believed he had 'plugged' de Coster, and that he himself was 'nuts'!

Worse still; during the hours when he had been lying on the camp-bed, listening to the noises in the kitchen, he had almost fancied now and then that he was back in his bedroom in Groningen, listening to his wife and the servant chattering away downstairs. They had the same way of making desultory remarks as they went about their tasks, and they too voiced their opinions on people, as if they knew about everything under the sun.

As regards Louis, however, Goin was probably right. Louis was a young fellow who fancied himself a mastermind – but as often as not had no real idea what he was doing.

Never had Kees had such a sense of uplift as now, pacing the platform, smoking a cigar, occasionally pausing to contemplate the poster of a beauty spot. From a lone eminence he looked down on the lesser breeds of men like Louis, Goin, and even Julius de Coster, mere pretentious windbags!

He was certain, if he bought any of those papers at the bookstall, to find something – perhaps a whole column – about himself. Very likely there would be another photograph as well. And people were shaking in their shoes at the thought that the famous 'maniac of Amsterdam' was at large in their midst.

Calmly he walked to the booking-office, bought a second-class ticket, and waited on the platform for the train that would take him to Paris, where Superintendent Lucas was hunting high and low for him.

What better proof could there be that he was cleverer, more resourceful, than all of them? He had in mind an even bolder step: nothing short of calling on Jeanne – just because it was so risky, the one thing he shouldn't do!

In any case, he had to see her; there were things that needed straightening out between them.

The train came in. As chance would have it, he stepped into a carriage where two women from the country, in dark dresses, were retailing the gossip of their respective villages: neighbours' illnesses and recent deaths. As, on his best behaviour, he watched them from his corner, he had a fantastic impulse to address them.

'Let me introduce myself, ladies. I'm Kees Popinga, the maniac of Amsterdam!'

Of course he didn't say it. But several times it was on the tip of his tongue, and he chuckled inwardly at the thought of the scene that would ensue. All the same, when they reached Paris he gallantly got down their luggage from the rack and, when they thanked him, replied politely, though with an ironic twinkle in his eye:

'Don't mention it!'

When all was said and done, this was exactly what he had wanted all along: to be alone, absolutely alone, in knowing what he knew; to be agreeably conscious of being Kees Popinga as he mixed with the crowd and rubbed shoulders with people who didn't know him from Adam and imagined all sorts of absurd things, different in each case, about him.

Those two good ladies, for instance – for them he was 'such a nice man, a real gentleman; what a pity there's so few like him nowadays!' While for Rose – as a matter of fact she'd kept her opinion of him to herself, but he suspected that, through lack of imagination, she regarded him with contempt.

It was a pleasure to be back in the cheerful streets of Paris, with buses, taxis and crowds of people hurrying in quest of heaven knew what – nothing at all, most likely. He, anyhow, had no need to hurry. Picratts never closed before 3 a.m. and, assuming Jeanne came out alone, she wouldn't be at her place before a quarter past.

What could have possessed him to let the opportunity go by that night they'd spent together at the hotel? Whereas now, the mere thought of her . . . ! Still, there had been a change; now that she *knew*, it was worth his while to master her, perhaps to frighten her a little, for she was too intelligent to turn him down light-heartedly as that fool Pamela had done.

Meanwhile, to fill the empty hours ahead, he went up to a policeman and asked the way to the headquarters of the Police Judiciaire. Wasn't it natural enough that this should interest him, since whenever there was a reference to him in the papers, the name of Superintendent Lucas of the Police Judiciaire invariably cropped up? It was a satisfaction to him to discover the Quai des Orfèvres and to make out, inscribed above an ill-lit portico, the words: Police Judiciaire. More satisfactory still if he could have had a glimpse of the superintendent himself – but that was too much to hope for.

So he contented himself with sitting for some moments on the Seine parapet and gazing up at the first-floor windows, behind which lamps were still alight. Beyond the massive archway, in the dark courtyard, two police cars and a prisoners' van were drawn up.

He moved away regretfully. He'd have liked to go inside and have a close-up view. At the Place Saint-Michel he cast a last backward glance before inquiring – of a policeman again – the way to Montmartre. He'd have been quite capable of asking his way even if he knew it for the mere joy of addressing a constable and chuckling to himself: 'If he only knew . . . !'

It was out of the question walking the streets till three in the morning, and he broke his progress to Montmartre by halts at small bars on the way. Round each crescent-shaped counter he found a little group of night-birds whose lives seemed for the moment in abeyance. Some were sipping coffee, staring listlessly in front of them; others, who had finished their drinks, were leaning on the counter, their eyes so vacant that one wondered if ever, and by what stroke of magic, they would wake to life again. In one of these bars the sight of a little girl with a basket of violets reminded him of Christmas Eve and the two visits Jeanne had paid him as he waited in the *café-tabac*.

Yes, Goin might well be right. It was Jeanne who had persuaded Louis to take an interest in him. Why had she done so? Had he impressed her somehow? Was it because he hadn't behaved to her as other men behaved? Or that she was perversely drawn to him because of what he'd done to Pamela?

Kees rejected pity as an explanation, not only because he wasn't out for pity, but because Jeanne wasn't the woman to feel it.

'Another hour to go!' he muttered impatiently.

As the night wore on he found himself thinking more and more about Jeanne, and he tried to picture what would happen when they met. So far he had been drinking mineral water; now he took to brandy, and he felt the fever rising in his blood.

At two-thirty, catching sight of his face in a mirror, he suddenly thought: 'The queer thing is that nobody in the world knows how it will turn out. Not even I. Not even Jeanne, who must be beginning to think about going home. Louis is in Marseilles. Goin and his sister are asleep, with no idea the bird has flown! Nobody knows . . .'

He asked the waiter for a paper and was vexed to find no mention of him till the fifth page, and only a few lines there. Still more vexing, all they found to say was the usual vague announcement that Superintendent Lucas was 'prosecuting his inquiry with vigour and an early arrest may be expected'.

This fellow Lucas was another one who thought himself mighty clever, but knew absolutely nothing. Though, of course, he might have had that bit about an 'early arrest' put in just to scare Kees into some foolish move.

Anyhow, this omniscience of the superintendent would very soon be put to the test! Kees asked – of a policeman, naturally – the way to the Rue Fromentin, and paced it several times, peering into every doorway and dark corner to see if there were anyone on the watch in the neighbourhood of No. 13. There was no one.

Which meant that nobody'd guessed he'd call on Jeanne tonight! In other words, Lucas didn't understand; Popinga still had the upper hand. What a facer it would be for that cocksure superintendent if something else, something sensational, happened in the next few hours! And what would the newspapers find to say about it – those newspapers that printed so docilely his banal reassurances?

It came to this. The more things he did, the more the police would be handicapped, for each new act of his would set them a new problem: they'd lose themselves in theories and end up by being completely fogged. Yes, the great thing was to keep them guessing. And, after all, there was nothing to prevent him 'doing things'. Just now, for instance, in the train, what had there been to prevent him from assaulting those two women, pulling the communication cord, and quietly stepping out of the train while people were rushing up and down the corridors?

He had no trouble in finding the cabaret where he had spent his first hours in Paris. He strolled up and down the street, waiting for closing time. Really, when he arrived in Paris, he hadn't had time to think things over, and anyhow he didn't know the ropes. Now he felt almost sorry for the novice who had alighted from the train at the Gare du Nord, promptly gone to a cabaret, ordered champagne, and started confiding in a wench like Jeanne.

Some women came out of the cabaret. They were of the

same type as Jeanne, but she was not amongst them. This reminded him of an annoying possibility; she might have a man in tow when she came out – in which case he would have to postpone action, perhaps till the following day.

No, there she was – alone! She was wearing her squirrel coat, with a bunch of violets pinned to the lapel. Her absurdly high heels clicked on the pavement.

She seemed to feel the cold and walked as fast as she could, hugging the house-fronts, without a glance to either side, like someone who every day at the same hour takes the same route.

Kees kept a little behind her, on the opposite pavement; he felt sure now she would not escape him.

All the same, he had an anxious moment when he saw her entering one of the few bars that remained open. A moment later, peeping through the window, he saw to his relief that she was alone, munching a croissant that now and again she dipped in a cup of café-au-lait.

Evidently no one had invited her to supper. So far, so good. As she drank the coffee her eyes had that far-away look he had noticed in the eyes of most of those who snatch a meal in such places. She took some money from her bag, paid, and went out at once.

He waited till she had rung at her door; then, while the concierge was setting in motion the mechanism that opened it from her room, stepped to Jeanne's side without a word. She gave a slight start but made no sound, though he seemed to catch a glint of fear in the greenish eyes. Then with a slight lift of her shoulders she stood aside to let him enter.

The lift was so small that their shoulders touched. It was Jeanne who pressed the button and, on the landing, sent it down again. As she was taking out her latch-key, she spoke at last.

'What do you want to tell Louis?'

He merely smiled at her, and she dropped her eyes, for she

guessed he had seen through her ruse. Only as they stepped into the flat did Kees reply:

'I haven't come to see Louis. He's in Marseilles.'

'Did Goin tell you?'

'No.'

She had shut the door and turned on the light in the hall. It was a three-room flat with a bathroom, furnished in an old-fashioned style with a profusion of would-be Persian rugs and quantities of shoddy bric-à-brac. A pair of satin slippers lay on the drawing-room floor, and on the table was a half-empty bottle of wine beside a half-eaten sandwich.

'Why have you come here?' she asked.

He gave no answer. He was busy making sure her eyes were green, as he remembered them, and he had an impression that fear had made them greener still.

'I might have shouted to the concierge.'

'Why should you?'

He seemed to feel quite at home here, so much so that, after taking off his overcoat, he tilted the bottle to his lips and drank some of the wine. After that, he opened a door, which proved to be that of the bedroom. Noticing a telephone on the bedside table, he thought: 'Must keep an eye on that,' but already Jeanne had intercepted his glance and guessed his thought.

It was good sport having to deal with somebody like her, quick in the uptake and so self-controlled that only the faintest changes of expression betrayed her feelings.

'Won't you undress?' he asked as he took off his collar and tie.

She still had her fur coat on. Suddenly, with a little fatalistic gesture, she slipped it off.

'When I found out that Louis was going to Marseilles,' he said, 'I thought it was too good a chance to miss ... Whose portrait is that over the bed?'

'My father's.'

'A handsome man. That moustache of his, especially, is quite impressive!'

He settled into a small Louis XVI armchair to take off his shoes. Jeanne, however, had stopped undressing. After pacing to and fro for some moments she halted in the middle of the room and said:

'You're not thinking of staying here, are you?'

'Till tomorrow anyhow.'

'I'm sorry, but it's out of the question.'

She had pluck. But she couldn't keep her eyes from straying now and then to the telephone. Especially as, instead of answering, he laughed and took off his second shoe.

'Did you hear what I said?'

'I heard it, but I don't see why you're making all this fuss. It won't be the first night we spend in bed together, will it? That other night I was dog-tired. And, of course, I didn't really know you. Since then I've regretted . . .'

He remained seated, well pleased with himself, but conscious of a flutter of emotion that made his voice less steady.

'Listen!' she said gravely. 'I didn't want to make a scene just now when we came in, and have the concierge and all the other tenants turning out. I know the risks you're running. But you've got to put your clothes on again – at once! And – clear out of here! Surely you're not so crazy as to imagine I'll . . . do what you want, now that . . .' She paused.

'Now that what?'

'Oh, nothing.'

'Now that you know. That's what you mean, eh? Now you know what happened to Pamela. Out with it, Jeanne! I'm right aren't I? Really, I'm enjoying this immensely. For the last three days I've been wondering how you felt about it.'

'Very flattering, I'm sure!'

'Yes, and I told myself, "She's not like the others. She's no fool. She understands . . ."'

'Very likely – but you've got to clear out all the same.'

'And suppose I don't?'

He rose and faced her, standing in his socks, his collar-stud pushed forward by his Adam's-apple.

'Then you'll get what's coming to you.'

In her hand was a small revolver with a mother-o'-pearl grip, which she had snatched out of a drawer. Though it was not pointed at him, the way she held it was far from reassuring.

'You'd shoot, would you?'

'I don't know . . . Quite likely.'

'Why? Yes, I ask you why tonight you're making all this fuss. The first time it was I who didn't feel like it.'

'Will you leave my flat, please?'

She was edging her way towards the telephone, but there was a clumsiness in her movements that betrayed the alarm she was trying to conceal. And perhaps it was this glimpse of her panic that set him off, and played havoc with his self-control. But even so, he did not lose his sense of stagecraft. Letting his head droop, he murmured sadly:

'How can you be so unkind, Jeanne? Don't you realize I've nobody in the world who understands me except you, and –'

'Don't come near me!'

'All right, I won't if you don't want me to. But do please listen to what I have to say. I know that Goin and his sister wanted to hand me over to the police.'

'Who told you that?' she asked vehemently.

'I overheard them talking. And I also learnt that Louis has an idea of squeezing money out of me.'

'That's not true.'

'It is true. He may not have said so to you, but he told Goin, and Goin repeated it to his sister. I heard every word they said. So I climbed out of the window – and here I am!'

Evidently she was taken aback, and her attitude seemed less

hostile now; she gazed for some moments at the floor, thinking it over. Keenly observing the play of emotions on her face, he continued:

'And it's obvious that you were in with them – you knew all about their dirty schemes. That's why you got out your revolver.'

'No, that wasn't the reason.' Her voice rang true; she looked him in the eyes.

'Then – why?'

'Don't you understand?'

'You mean you're afraid of me?'

'No.'

'Well then?'

'That's enough.'

He had managed to take three steps towards her. Another two, and she would be within reach. Now there was no retreating. He hadn't settled what he was going to do, but he knew that whatever was to happen was, at this moment, under way.

'I wonder if it's any good my telling you . . .'

'Be quiet!'

'If she hadn't been such a damned fool . . .'

'Didn't I tell you to be quiet!'

In her exasperation she waved her arm, which meant that, for a brief moment, the revolver was no longer pointing at him. That was enough. Kees was on her like a flash; sent her sprawling across the bed; wrenched the weapon from her grip. With his left hand he caught up the pillow and crammed it over her face to stifle her cries; then leant on it with all his weight.

'Promise you won't call for help!'

She was strongly built and put up a good fight. In the course of it the pillow slipped off her face and he struck her on the head with the butt of the revolver several times – how many times he had no idea, so intent was he on watching for the moment when she ceased to struggle.

When, after washing his hands, which had some traces of blood on them, he started putting on his shoes, he was as calm as after the Pamela affair. But now it was a pensive calm tinged with a vague regret. Which was apparent when he had finished dressing and, going up to the bed, stroked Jeanne's red hair, and murmured:

'Very clever of you, wasn't it!'

Not till he was outside the flat and closed the door behind him did a consoling thought come to his mind. 'That's settled it, anyhow!' Nobody else, he knew, would have understood what he meant by that. Indeed, he himself could have hardly put into words what it was that was 'settled'. It was everything – everything that had linked his life till now with the lives of other men. Henceforth he was alone, an outlaw, with the whole world against him!

On the ground floor he had a moment of dismay. The street door was locked and, not knowing the ways of Paris, he had no idea how to get it opened for him. A cold sweat broke out on his forehead, and for a moment he thought of retiring to the top floor and waiting there till people living in the building came down in the morning.

But just then, as luck would have it, someone rang, and the door opened with a click. A man and a woman stepped inside, uttering a startled exclamation as a dark form brushed past them into the street. More people who would have a tale to tell the police about him on the following day!

Montmartre was at its calmest; the neon lights outside the cabarets had been switched off. There were still a few taxis prowling about, however, and a driver hailed him. But why take a taxi when he had nowhere to go?

Something unpleasant was hovering in the background of

his mind – a picture of Jeanne lying helpless on the bed, unconscious still, perhaps. Yes, something must be done about it. He
hailed a passing taxi; had trouble in explaining what he wanted.

'Listen! Will you drive to 13, Rue Fromentin? Go straight up
to Mademoiselle Rozier's flat on the third floor. She wants a
taxi to take her to the station immediately. Here's twenty
francs in advance.'

Catching a look of suspicion on the man's face, he added
hastily:

'It's quite OK. The lady has a train to catch.'

The man took the money and drove off, while Kees strode
rapidly towards the centre of the city. What could it matter to
him whether the police got busy a few hours earlier or later,
since he was certain to outwit them anyhow?

It would be interesting to see if Jeanne gave a full description
of him, and joined forces with the police. Improbable as it was,
something told him that she wouldn't.

He was extraordinarily tired and felt like sleeping twelve, or
for that matter twenty-four, hours on end, as indeed he had
been doing recently. The trouble was that if he went to an
hotel they'd make him fill up forms and might even want him
to show identity papers. Luckily Jeanne had taught him how
to turn that difficulty.

He went on walking the streets, taking long strides, until
he saw a belated prostitute still on the prowl. He beckoned to
her and had her lead him to an hotel. Once they were in the
bedroom he took the precaution of slipping his money under
the pillow.

'You're a foreigner, aren't you?'

'Don't bother! I want to sleep. Here's a hundred francs for
you. Now leave me in peace, please.'

No sooner had his eyes closed than he was back in Groningen, with Mum dressing in front of the glass. He saw her
peer into it and squeeze a tiny pimple. Meanwhile the maid

was making the usual din in the kitchen below. Only now the maid was Rose. And, when, a few minutes later, he came downstairs and crept up behind her, she wagged a reproving finger at him.

'If you won't behave, I'm off!'

Then a voice whispered in his ear:

'Take care. That tin marked *Salt* has sugar in it. It doesn't go with oxtail soup.'

The voice sounded familiar, yet he couldn't place it. Suddenly it dawned on him; that was Jeanne who had spoken to him, and he was standing collarless, shoeless, in the middle of the kitchen – and there was a party going on in his house. She laughed and started scolding him, with a note of playful affection in her voice.

'Buck up and get dressed, you lazybones! Don't you know they'll recognize you?'

7

How Kees Popinga pitched his wandering tent, and how he thought fit to help the French police with their inquiries

You may start from almost any detail, however trivial, and often find it leading, without any conscious effort on your part, to discoveries of prime importance.

Since his earliest days, Kees had had a habit of inspecting his face each morning in the glass with extreme intentness. This morning was no exception, and it struck him that his failure to shave since leaving Holland, though the growth of hair was neither plentiful nor dark, seriously detracted from his appearance.

He turned towards the bed, on the edge of which a woman was sitting, putting on her stockings.

'As soon as you're dressed, please go out and buy me a safety-razor, a shaving-brush, a stick of shaving-soap and a toothbrush.'

As he had given her the money in advance, he ran the risk that she wouldn't return. As it turned out, she was honest, and even insisted on giving an exact account of her expenditure and returning the change. After that, not knowing whether he wanted her to stay or to leave him, and not daring to ask, she sat down on the bed and watched him shaving.

The hotel in which they were was much inferior to the one in the Rue Victor-Massé, to which it stood in exactly the same relation as the woman on the bed to Jeanne – that is to say, two or three grades lower.

On the other hand, this woman, whose name Kees didn't

know, seemed genuinely anxious to please him, and kept on trying to discover his tastes and preferences.

'You're one of the melancholy sort, aren't you? I know what it is; you've been crossed in love.' She had the tone, at once assured and tentative, of a professional fortune-teller.

'What gives you that idea?' he asked as he went on lathering his chin.

'Because I'm getting to understand men. How old should you say I am? Well, I'm thirty-eight, dearie, though I know I don't look my age. So, you see, I've often come across fellows like you who take a girl to an hotel and don't do anything. Sooner or later most of 'em start telling you about themselves, all the rotten luck they've had. That's where girls like us come in handy. We know how to listen, and what they say to us don't matter.'

There was a pleasant homeliness about the scene: Kees bare from the waist up, his braces dangling round his calves, and the woman amiably discoursing to pass away the time till he had finished dressing. Queerly enough, though he duly noted her opinion that he was 'of the melancholy sort' – yet another character that was being foisted on him, and due to be recorded in his notebook – he very soon ceased listening to what she said.

The razor had switched his thoughts on to a new track, and he was wondering if he shouldn't buy a small case in which to keep his few belongings. For, if he took a room for the night in a better-class hotel, the lack of any luggage might draw attention to him. With a case in his hand he could pass for a commercial traveller. The trouble would be to know what to do with it in the day time – though, of course, he could leave it at a railway cloakroom, or in a café.

Whatever he did, one thing he was resolved on: never to sleep two nights running at the same place. He remembered that suspects often let themselves get caught because of some small incriminating detail noted by those with whom they came in contact.

'No case!' he murmured to himself as he carefully wiped the razor and wrapped it in a piece of newspaper. Not to mention that he might come to be known as 'the man with the case', and this harmless adjunct might well lead to his detection.

His superiority over the ruck of fugitives from justice – robbers, murderers, or swindlers, whose exploits he had read of in the papers – consisted in this: that he was able to review his position coolly, with complete detachment – exactly as in the past he had handled business deals at de Coster's – as if nothing in it concerned him personally.

In fact, he treated it much like a chess problem, and sought the solution for the solution's sake. Abruptly he turned to the woman seated on the bed.

'Tell me! In hotels of this sort do they ask for one's identity papers?'

'Never. Sometimes they make you sign in the register. And once in a while the cops turn up in the middle of the night and haul everybody out of bed. They usually do that when there's same foreign VIP visiting Paris and they're afraid of bombs being thrown.'

After carefully wrapping up the shaving-brush, tooth-brush, and shaving-soap, Kees stowed them in his overcoat pocket, along with the red notebook and a pencil – the meagre total of his personal effects. But, after all, it made things simpler, having no encumbrances. He could move about freely, sleeping each night in a different hotel – or, better still, in a different part of Paris. Of course, there was always the chance of one of those police raids the woman had talked about, but he reckoned it was a hundred to one against his being involved in one.

'Will you take me out to lunch?' she asked.

'Well, to tell the truth, I'd rather not.'

'That's quite all right. I only mentioned it as I thought you might like company. Then you don't want me any longer?'

'No.'

They parted on the pavement in a street cluttered up with costermongers' barrows. Kees had no watch, but he saw the time by a clock at the end of the street; it was a quarter past twelve.

He rather liked this part of Paris; it was as densely populated as anyone could wish, teeming with all different sorts of people, and well supplied with little bars, all of which were crowded.

He summed up his position. 'I've roughly three thousand francs left, which should keep me going for a month or so – time enough to look round and find a way of getting some more money.'

And of a sudden he turned thrifty, for this money, to which until now he'd hardly given a thought, had become of extreme importance – like the razor in his pocket, the absence of a care; like every detail of the scheme of life he was engaged in drawing up.

In pursuance of this plan he spent nearly an hour studying the map of Paris posted at the entrance of a Métro station. He had a remarkably good memory for topography, and had very soon memorized the various districts, boulevards, and principal streets, so thoroughly that he would be able to find his way unaided, through almost any part of Paris.

He wasn't hungry, and his lunch consisted of two large glasses of milk and some croissants. After which he proceeded to the boulevards, where the afternoon papers were just coming on sale, and bought a copy of each.

Though he had done his best to keep his mind off Jeanne, he had been worrying over her all the morning. There was bound to be something about her in the papers, and he scanned them eagerly for news of her condition. To his amazement and disgust, there was a not a line relating to her. Nor was there anything about himself. It seemed as if the Pamela affair had been completely forgotten; on the other hand, there was a long account of a mysterious crime that had taken place on the Paris–Basel express.

Obviously, if Jeanne was dead, the papers would have some mention of it ... But would they? Suppose the police had purposely had the news suppressed, in order to throw dust in his eyes or to lure him on to some rash act? If only he could have had a glimpse, even across a window, of that fellow Lucas! Then he'd have had something to go on; he could at least have judged the sort of man he had to deal with, and thus be able to foresee to some extent his tactics.

Well, it couldn't be helped! One thing at least he could do without any great risk, as, fortunately enough, Jeanne had a telephone on her bedside table.

He entered a café, found her number, and called it. An unknown voice, which sounded like an elderly woman's, asked him what he wanted.

'Can I speak to Mademoiselle Rozier?' he asked.

'What name, please?'

'Oh, just say one of her friends.'

So far so good. Anyhow, she wasn't dead. There was a short silence. Then:

'Hello! I'm afraid you can't speak to her just now. She's not very well. Can I give a message?'

'Not seriously ill, I hope?'

'No, not very seriously, but ...'

That was enough. He hung up, went back to the restaurant, and sat down at one of the tables. A quarter of an hour later he asked for writing paper, a pen, and ink.

He was in a temper, but none the less gave careful thought to what he was to say. After some minutes he started writing in a bold, clear hand:

To Superintendent Lucas.

Sir, I feel it is my duty to report to you that another incident took place last night which has its bearing on the Popinga case. It might be well if you called at Mlle Rozier's flat in the Rue Fromentin and asked her how she comes to be in her present state.

He paused, wondering if he should give any further information. Then a thought of Goin and his sister crossed his mind, and he took up the pen again, chuckling to himself.

I will also take this opportunity of giving the French police a helping hand; they have shown so much interest in me that I feel I owe this to them. You can, in the very near future, lay hands on a gang of motor-thieves operating on a big scale. This is the gang which on Christmas Eve stole three cars in the Montmartre district.

I would advise you to detail some of your men to watch the 'Goin and Boret' garage at Juvisy. There is no point in taking action tonight or tomorrow night, as nothing will happen, the leader of the gang being absent in Marseilles. But you will be well advised to have your men there on the following nights, and I shall be greatly surprised if you fail to make a haul before the new year.

I remain, Sir, Your most obedient servant,

Kees Popinga

He read the letter over with satisfaction, stuck down the envelope, wrote the address, and called the waiter.

'If I post a letter now, when will it be delivered?'

'In Paris? Tomorrow morning. But if you send it express it should be delivered within two hours.'

Another discovery that Kees was making, for he hadn't known that letters can be sent in Paris by pneumatic tube. He went to the nearest post office, bought the necessary stamp, and posted his letter. After that he walked briskly towards another part of Paris, for he had deliberately used notepaper headed with the name of the café where the letter was written.

It was four o'clock. Haloes of mist hung round the street-lamps, and the weather was turning cold again. Walking straight ahead, he came to the Seine at the exact point where he had reckoned to strike it – beside the Pont Neuf, which he crossed.

He was not walking aimlessly; he had something definite in view. Now that he had disposed of his more pressing business, he felt need for relaxation, and what could be better than a game of chess?

Suppose, he asked himself, a newcomer to Groningen, knowing nobody, wanted to find someone to play chess with, where would he stand the best chance of doing so? The answer was obvious: at the big café near the University, patronized mainly by students.

There was every likelihood it was the same in Paris. Accordingly, he made his way to the Latin Quarter and turned into its main street, the Boulevard Saint-Michel. At first he felt rather lost – it was so different from the quiet thoroughfares of Groningen – but he refused to be discouraged.

He peeped into a dozen or more cafés without seeing any sign of games being played; one had the impression that the people at the tables had dropped in merely for a drink.

Then, on the far side of the boulevard, he noticed a big brasserie, on the first floor of which dim forms could be seen moving to and fro behind the curtains, some of them with billiard cues.

He felt as pleased with himself as if he'd just won a bet. A moment later he was even more gratified, for, when he had climbed to the first floor and entered a huge, barn-like room in which green-shaded lamps hung in the smoky air above ten or a dozen billiard-tables, he saw quite a number of people playing cards, backgammon, and chess.

Methodically as at his chess club he took off his heavy over-coat and hung it on a peg, went to a basin and washed his hands, brushed his hair, cleaned his nails, then sat down beside two young men who were playing chess, and ordered a glass of beer and a cigar.

A pity he had resolved never to show up twice at the same spot, for this would have been an ideal place in which to spend his afternoons. For one thing, there were no women – which was just as well! – and the majority of those present were students, easy-going youngsters who played billiards in their shirtsleeves.

One of the two chess-players was Japanese with horn-rimmed spectacles; the other a tall, fair, pink-cheeked young man, whose facial expressions clearly showed what he was feeling.

Just as he always did at Groningen, Kees took from his pocket his gold-rimmed glasses and wiped them before putting them on. Thereafter minute followed minute during which he did no more than gaze at the chessboard, whose layout imprinted itself on his memory as precisely as the plan of Paris he had studied earlier in the day.

It was extraordinarily like Groningen! There was the same smell in the room, a mingled odour of beer, tobacco smoke and sawdust. The waiter too had the same habit; on his way to other tables he would halt behind the chess-players and watch a fragment of the game with a critical, usually disapproving eye.

Under such conditions Kees was capable of staying for a long while without moving, without even uncrossing his legs, while the ash of his cigar lengthened to an inch or more. It was only towards the end of the game, when the Japanese had been eyeing the chessboard ruefully for a good ten minutes without venturing on a move, that he flicked the ash from his cigar and said quietly:

'So you win in two moves, don't you?'

The Japanese gazed at him dumbfounded, all the more so because he had been quite convinced the game was lost. His opponent was no less taken aback, for he saw no conceivable way in which he could be checkmated, as the game stood.

There was a short silence. The Japanese reached towards his castle, raised it gingerly as if it had been red-hot, and looked inquiringly at Kees, while the fair young man scanned the board again and sighed:

'Do you know, I really don't see how . . .'

'Will you permit me?'

The yellow man nodded. The other looked on sceptically.

'I move the knight here. What do you do now?'

Without stopping to think, the fair young man replied:

'I take it with my rook, of course.'

'Quite so. Then I move my queen two squares forward. What do you do now?'

This time the young man found nothing to say, stayed for a moment at a loss, then moved his king back a square.

'That settles it. I move my queen one square forward, and you're mated. Fairly obvious, wasn't it?'

In such cases he always assumed a modest demeanour, though his face beamed with satisfaction. The two young men were so much impressed that they didn't think of starting another game.

The Japanese, however, who had been applying his mind to understanding Kees's tactics, looked up and said:

'Like a game, sir?'

'Yes, take my place,' the other man suggested.'

'Not a bit of it! Look here, if you feel like it, I'll take you both on at the same time. Each of you will have a separate board, of course.'

When, as he now did, he rubbed his hands together, one couldn't help noticing how finely shaped they were – if a shade too plump – and how white and smooth the skin.

'Waiter, bring another set of chessmen and a board.'

Superintendent Lucas hadn't got the express letter yet, but by the time the two games were over it should have reached him. In which case, he would probably rush round at once to Jeanne's flat.

The two young men were a little intimidated, especially as Popinga, who was on the wall-sofa facing them with the two chessboards before him, made a point of following with his eyes a game of billiards that was going on at a table a few yards off, as well as the two games of chess in progress. He was quite aware of the effect he was producing, and enjoyed it.

He played without hesitating between moves, whereas his opponents spent some time thinking theirs out; especially the Japanese, who was set on winning.

Meanwhile Kees was wondering if there was any way of getting a list of the Paris cafés at which chess is played. There must be quite a number of them, he supposed, for when studying the map of Paris he had made a discovery. In Groningen, as in most towns, there is one central district, and only one, round which the residential and working-class quarters are grouped like the flesh of a fruit around the stone.

But Kees had noticed that in Paris there are several such centres; indeed, each district has, so to speak, a local nucleus, complete with cafés, picture-houses, dancing-halls, and a shopping-quarter.

From which it followed that a chess-player residing in, say, the Grenelle district wouldn't dream of coming all the way to the Boulevard Saint-Michel for a game; nor would a resident of the Parc Montsouris. So all he had to do was to keep his eyes open; in each district he would find what he was after.

'I say!' he suddenly exclaimed with feigned embarrassment. 'You'd better take that bishop back. If you don't, you'll get yourself checkmated by my queen.'

The fair young man, whom he was addressing, blushed and stammered:

'But I . . . I've moved it. I can't take it back.'

'Please do so. It was just an oversight.'

From the corner of an eye the Japanese was watching his friend's game, so as to avoid making the same mistakes.

'You're students, aren't you. What's your subject?'

'Medicine,' said the Japanese.

His friend was training to be a dentist – a profession that would suit him well.

For all the concentration the Japanese brought to his game, he was the first to succumb. The other young man made desperate efforts, but survived him only by a few minutes.

Kees felt called on to offer them drinks.

'Certainly not,' said the fair man. 'You must have one with us.'

'We're the losers,' the Japanese pointed out.

Nevertheless, Kees insisted on standing the drinks, then lit another cigar and leant back on the wall-sofa.

'The great thing, you know, is to keep a clear idea in your head of the layout of all the chessmen on the board, and not to forget that the bishop protects the queen, the queen protects the knight, and . . .' He all but added: 'And Louis must have had a wire from Jeanne and is already on his way back from Marseilles. And, at this moment, very likely, Superintendent Lucas is calling on Jeanne, who must be wondering what on earth he's come for. And, at Juvisy, Goin is itching to ring her up, but doesn't dare, and Rose . . .'

He went on hastily:

'Also one should study the other fellow's method – and have none oneself. Suppose I'd had a method . . . I might have beaten one of you, but the other would have spotted my tactics and quite possibly got the better of me . . .'

He was thoroughly enjoying himself. So much so that when the two young men, after thanking him profusely, went away, he lingered on, puffing his cigar, his thumbs stuck in the arm-holes of his waistcoat, watching a distant game of billiards and half inclined to chip in, as he had done with the chess-players.

For at billiards, too, he could have brought it off as he had done at chess; could have taken the cue from one of the players and knocked up a break of fifty right away.

One thing that his opponents hadn't noticed during the game of chess was that on the far side of the room, facing him, the wall was panelled with mirrors. The lighting was far from bright and the air thick with pipe and cigarette smoke, so that all Kees could see of his reflected self was a blurred, rather enigmatic visage; but he observed it with complacence, pursing his lips on his cigar.

A clock with a garishly white dial pointed to six o'clock. To pass the time he got out his notebook and pondered lengthily before starting to write.

For he had discovered that there were a great number of hours to get through every day, even when one put in the maximum of sleep. He couldn't roam the streets for more than three or four hours on end; in the long run it was not only tiring but, in the end, depressing. If he was to keep himself physically and mentally fit, what he needed was regular relaxation like that game of chess, and he resolved to organize his days accordingly.

After a while he started writing:

> *Tuesday, 28 December. Left Juvisy by the window. Two women in train. Saw Jeanne at her flat; she didn't laugh. As a precaution stunned her slightly. Certain I shall see her again.*

Wednesday, 29 December. Slept with woman in hotel, Faubourg Montmartre; forgot to ask her name. She took me for a 'melancholy sort'. Bought toilet requisites. Wrote to Superintendent Lucas and played chess. In excellent form.

Brief, but adequate. It sufficed to recall to his mind all his experiences and impressions of the last forty-eight hours, including the decision he had come to in the morning about the case. He had refrained from buying one so as to avoid getting known as 'the man with the case'. In fact, anything that might make him conspicuous, any idiosyncrasy, must be avoided. And now, observing himself in the glass, he realized that his cigar was a characteristic. Those two young men would certainly remember it; so would the waiter at the café where he'd written his letter. For, on looking round the room, he noticed that hardly anybody – perhaps two of the fifty men in it – was smoking a cigar.

Jeanne knew he was a cigar-smoker; so did Goin, and the head waiter at Picratts. The woman he'd parted company with at noon had noticed it.

That meant that, if he didn't wish to become known as 'the man with the cigar', he must take to smoking cigarettes, or a pipe. It went against the grain, as a cigar was, so to speak, a facet of his personality; but, now that his mind was made up, he promptly crushed out what remained of the cigar and filled the ugly little pipe he'd bought at Juvisy.

He felt certain that by now Lucas was conducting his inquiry at Jeanne's place, questioning the concierge and quite likely the two people he had brushed against in the doorway. It would be quite amusing to ring him up and say:

'Is that Superintendent Lucas? Kees Popinga speaking. Well, what do you think of the tip I gave you? Anyhow, you must agree it was a sporting thing to do, giving you points like that . . .'

No, that would be foolhardy. He had a suspicion that the police could trace telephone calls right away. However, this did not deter him from indulging in a little joke. In a corner of the room was a telephone box. He entered it and rang up the three newspapers which had published the longest articles about him. When calling the last one, he even asked to speak to the member of the staff who had signed the article.

'Listen! Kees Popinga committed another crime last night. You can check up on it if you go to No. 13, Rue Fromentin. Yes? What's that?'

At the other end of the line a voice inquired:

'Who's speaking? Is that you, Marchandeau?'

Evidently they took him for one of their usual informants!

'Of course not, I'm not Marchandeau. This is Popinga speaking. How do you do, Monsieur Saladin? Listen! I do wish you'd stop writing such balderdash about me, and, above all, saying that I'm mad.'

He took his hat and overcoat, went down the stairs and set out for the part of Paris in which he had decided to spend the night: the Bastille quarter.

It was not enough never to visit twice the same restaurant or hotel; he must also vary the class of place he patronized. Those two hotels he had slept at recently had been of a special category, and he could have sworn they'd go on looking for him in hotels of that type. In fact, he was certain that Lucas would have searches made in many of them during the coming night, expecting him to repeat himself – just as those two young chess-players had watched all the time for him to repeat the tactics they'd observed him using once.

So he decided to have a four- or five-franc meal at one of the small eating-houses in the slums round the Bastille, and to spend the night in an equally cheap hotel.

He had not yet made up his mind, however, whether to sleep alone, or, as he had done twice already, have a girl with him.

Walking slowly along the Rue Saint-Antoine, he applied his mind to the problem. He was well aware it was as dangerous as always smoking a cigar, or carrying a case; indeed more dangerous. The police would certainly record something of this sort in his dossier: *'Has a habit of spending his nights with women picked up in the street.'* And they would start keeping a watch on all the places where there were women on the game.

'Most imprudent,' he told himself.

And it would be almost as imprudent to play chess every day – even in different cafés – for sooner or later a further note would be recorded: *'Spends his afternoons playing chess at cafés in Paris and the suburbs.'*

That, anyhow, was what he, were he in the superintendent's place, would have noted; also that he always carried in his pockets a safety-razor, shaving-brush, and toothbrush. And suppose that something to that effect were published in the newspapers . . . ?

As he threaded his way through the crowd he couldn't help smiling at the thought of what would follow were such information published. For one thing, all the chess-players in the various cafés would start eyeing each other with suspicion, and perhaps, while they were at their games, the waiters would be rummaging in the pockets of their overcoats, especially the grey ones, to make sure there wasn't a razor or a shaving-brush in any of them. And the police would be inundated with telephone calls from women of the street, who would see Popinga in every man they happened to get off with!

Emphatically he told himself he must avoid doing any of these things. But even as he said it, he felt an almost uncontrollable impulse to do them – to behave in character with the personage thus depicted. He fought down the obsession, composed his thoughts as best he could, and decided to go to a cinema after dinner, to take his mind off such ideas.

He dined in a small restaurant where the meal cost five francs, but, as he couldn't bring himself to refuse the 'extras' on the menu, his bill came to eleven francs. He was served by a waitress in a white apron, and he wondered what she made of him. As a sort of test he gave her a five-franc tip.

Such lavishness, he supposed, would startle her, cause her to inspect him with attention, and even perhaps to link up this man in grey, who spoke with a foreign accent, with the 'Dutch maniac' about whom the newspapers had so much to tell.

Nothing of the sort! She pocketed the money and went on placidly with her work as if he'd given her merely fifty centimes or a franc.

There was a cinema just across the way: the Cinéma Saint-Paul. He took a seat in a box, as he had no objection to being well in view. The girl who showed him to his seat wore a red uniform much like that of the page boys at the Carlton Hotel in Amsterdam.

He tried the opposite method, and didn't give her the customary tip. But her only reaction was to grumble under her breath as she went away, and she took no more notice of him.

What had come over everyone today? It was as if he had been forgotten about, as if there were a conspiracy of silence concerning him. Jeanne hadn't called in the police. The newspapers had ceased talking about the case. Goin was lying low; Louis was in Marseilles, and that absurd woman this morning – what was it she said? That she'd met plenty of his sort before!

He seldom went to the pictures in Groningen; Mum regarded them as distressingly vulgar, and never failed to point out that the Thursday classical concerts for which they bought season tickets each winter provided relaxation at once adequate and refined.

At the Cinéma Saint-Paul there was an atmosphere of almost feverish excitement that was new to Kees. Never before had he been in a place of entertainment of this type, in which thousands of people are massed together, most of them sucking oranges or chewing sweets.

Behind him rose the gallery, tier upon tier, and, when he looked round, he saw hundreds of faces lit by the backwash of brightness from the screen. There was something about it all that fretted the nerves, and he half expected someone to jump up and shout:

'That's him! That's the madman from Amsterdam! That's the chap who . . . !'

In the boxes beside him were staid, portly matrons in fur coats, young women with plump, pink hands, and heavily built men, shopkeepers and business men of the Saint-Paul district.

In the interval a sort of dizziness came over him and he didn't dare to join the crowd of people flocking to the bars and lavatories. He watched the adverts, and the sight of a drawing-room suite reminded him of the one in Groningen which Mum had chosen after studying catalogues of all the furniture dealers in Holland.

What was Mum doing at this moment? What were her thoughts? She had spoken of 'loss of memory', probably because of that serial story in the *Telegraaf* which all the family had read, about a German soldier in the last war who as the result of shell shock had forgotten even his name, and came back after ten years to find his wife remarried and his children strangers to him.

And how about de Coster? He had talked of all sorts of things in the Saint George tavern, but had been cunning enough, drunk as he was, not to give away where he was going. From what Kees knew of him it was unlikely that he was in Paris. In London more probably; he knew London better. No doubt he'd got some money put by over there and would start another business with it, and be a rich man again . . .

As the audience were trooping back to their places the lights went out and a pale mauve glow rippled across the screen, while the orchestra played appropriately languorous music. Kees felt a little thrill of pleasure down his spine, and, when the music ended, there was a burst of applause in which he joined. But he was rather bored by the main feature which followed, about the troubles of a lawyer bound to professional secrecy.

In a box beside him a fat lady in a mink coat kept asking her husband:

'Why doesn't he tell the truth? What a fool the man is!'

The crowd surged out into the cold darkness of the street, where all the shops were shut and starters purred in the cars beside the kerb.

Popinga had noticed an hotel at the corner of the Rue de Birague, which, judging by its appearance, should be cheap and squalid – just the sort of hotel he wanted. His impression was confirmed when he saw a woman lurking in the darkness near the entrance.

Should he ask her to come in with him or not? Obviously, if he was to abide by his programme . . . Still, there could be no immediate danger; the police hadn't had time yet to note this 'habit' of his.

The truth was, he disliked being alone at night, and especially in the morning when he awoke. At such times he was reduced to studying himself in the glass, trying different facial expressions, thinking:

'Supposing I had a mouth like this . . . Or a nose like that . . . !'

After all, why not? Just this once more – if only to discover what sort of women haunted this queer little street. He walked past her, his hands in his pockets, with a deliberate air of casualness, and, at the last moment, as he'd expected, a timid voice inquired:

'Coming with me?'

He pretended to hesitate, looked round, and saw in the light of a streetlamp a young pale face, wisps of dark hair straggling from beneath a béret, a coat too thin for the season.

He thought quickly. 'She'll do!' By now he knew the procedure followed on such occasions. They walked past a small office in which a motherly-looking woman was playing patience.

'Number Seven,' she said.

Kees noted the coincidence; Room Seven again.

There was no dressing-room, but the washstand was curtained off. Without looking at the girl, Kees promptly disposed his razor, shaving-brush, and soap on it.

'Going to stay all night?' she asked.

'That's it!'

'Oh!' She didn't sound very pleased, but raised no objection. 'Do you live somewhere round here?' she asked.

'No.'

'A foreigner, aren't you?'

'How about *you*?'

'Oh, I'm from Brittany,' she said, as she took off her béret. 'You'll be nice to me, won't you? You were at the pictures, I saw you coming out.'

She was obviously making conversation, with the idea, perhaps, that this would please him, and it did make him feel more at ease in these discouraging surroundings. He undressed slowly, made sure the bed was relatively clean, then stretched himself on it with a sigh of content.

There was another woman he'd have greatly liked to set eyes on at this moment – Superintendent Lucas's wife. He wondered what the superintendent could be telling her about him, Kees Popinga, as he got into bed. For, after all, even he had to go to bed at night, like everyone else!

'Shall I leave the light on?'

She was so thin that he preferred to look away.

8

*Concerning the difficulty of getting rid of old
newspapers and the advantages of owning a
fountain-pen and a watch*

There was very little to record in the red notebook that
morning.

> *Her name is really Zulma! Gave her twenty francs and
> she didn't dare to protest. While I was dressing she
> remarked sadly:*
> *'I expect you don't like thin girls. If I'd known, I'd
> have brought my friend along; she's nice and plump.'*
> *Dirty feet.*

He also noted the necessity of buying a watch; when he was
out and about he could see the time on church clocks and in
cafés, but it was a nuisance not knowing it in the mornings.

This morning, for instance, when he went out, he was surprised to find that it was only eight; the noise and bustle of an
early-rising district had misled him.

While Zulma walked off, wrapped in her trusty black coat,
the shoulders of which were too wide for her, Kees went to a
newspaper kiosk, and what he saw there gave him a slight
shock. At last he was really in the limelight; two or three
whole columns were devoted to him on the front page of certain
papers. Though his portrait did not appear – probably because
they had already published the only one available – there were
pictures of Jeanne and of her room.

It cost him an effort not to buy all the newspapers *en bloc*
and rush into a café to read them. Really, it was enough to

make one lose one's head – the thought of all that mass of newsprint concerning him, giving impressions of the 'Popinga case' from different angles. People were brushing past him, buying papers and diving into a nearby Métro entrance.

He confined himself to the three leading dailies and went with them to a bar in the Place de la Bastille. Nobody could have guessed from his appearance the riot of emotions in his breast as he sipped a café-au-lait, read and re-read the articles, sometimes stung to the quick by what he read, sometimes exhilarated.

The next problem was how to cope with the printed matter in his possession. Nothing would persuade him to discard the articles he had just read, but he obviously couldn't walk the streets, his pockets bulging with newspapers.

He thought hard, then went down to the lavatory and cut out with his penknife all that dealt with him. The next thing was to get rid of what remained, and this took him nearly half an hour, as the sodden mass of paper wouldn't go down and he had to keep on pulling the chain and waiting for the cistern to fill again. When he reappeared at the bar they supposed he had been taken ill.

In the course of the morning, he bought the twenty-odd remaining newspapers in batches of three, so as not to attract attention. He read the first batch in a small bar at the corner of the Boulevard Henri IV and the Quais, and dropped the remnants into the river. The next batch he dealt with in a café on the Quai d'Austerlitz, and so he went on, following the river-bank and stopping every half-mile or so, till he reached the far end of the Quai de Bercy.

There, however, he found no café to his liking, and accordingly retraced his steps. Near the Gare de Lyon he lit on exactly the sort of place he wanted, a brasserie, and he settled down for the afternoon in a quiet corner under cover of the stove. Having left his fountain-pen in Groningen, he had bought another, and with it he set to work.

If he'd gone to the expense of buying a fountain-pen as well as a watch – the former had cost thirty-two francs and the latter eighty – it was because he had found it almost impossible to write with the pens provided by cafés for their customers.

So he merely asked for notepaper and began writing in a small, neat hand, for he knew he had a long spell of work before him and did not want to tire his wrist.

To the Editor.

This letter was to go to the leading Paris daily paper, which had devoted practically three columns to him, and whose correspondent had spent two days in Holland. If Kees selected this particular paper, it wasn't only because it had a large circulation, but also because it was the only one to show some intelligence in its heading.

> Pamela's murderer plays with the police by informing them about a new crime which they wouldn't otherwise have known about.

He had plenty of time to think out what to say. The stove was roaring like the one in Groningen, and the other customers, mostly people waiting for trains, made little noise.

Dear Sir, I must begin by apologizing for my French, but living in Holland for many years, I have not had much practice.

Suppose that in every newspaper people who were total strangers started alleging this and that about you, though nothing that they said was true and you were really quite different from the picture they presented – under these circumstances would you not feel aggrieved, justly aggrieved, and desire to set them right?

Your reporter went to Groningen and interviewed a number of persons; but these persons were not in a position to know the truth, or else told lies about me, deliberate in some cases, involuntary in others.

I wish to correct these false impressions, and will begin at the beginning, for I trust that you will publish this letter; it has at least the merit of being truthful, and it will show how a man can suffer by the careless talk of those who know, or claim to know, him.

The article begins with a description of my family, based on a statement made by my wife to your representative:

'I cannot understand what has happened, and it has come as a bolt from the blue. Kees comes of a very good family and had a first-class education. When we married, he was a quiet, sensible young man, whose fondest wish was to have a home of his own. We have been married for sixteen years, and I can say he was a model husband, the best of fathers. He had robust health, though perhaps I should mention that, during a severe frost last month, he slipped in the street and fell on his head. This may well have affected his brain and caused him to develop amnesia. In any case, when he acted as he did, he cannot have known what he was doing and should not be held responsible.'

Kees ordered another coffee and nearly asked for a cigar. Just in time he remembered his resolution, sighed, and filled a pipe. Then he reread the lines he had just written and set to refuting them.

I now proceed to make some comments on the passage quoted above.

(1) I do not come of a very good family. But you will understand why my wife, who is the daughter of a burgomaster, thought fit to mislead your representative on this point. My mother was a midwife and my father a builder. But it was my mother who kept the home together. When my father called on prospective customers, he spent

his time gossiping and drinking with them, and quite forgot to fix a price or have a proper contract drawn up; in fact, he was too sociable to be a success at business. But he refused to be discouraged, though sometimes he would admit he was 'too easygoing'.

My mother, however, was far from easygoing, and never a day passed without a domestic flare-up; it was particularly violent when my father had drunk more than usual. My mother would start screaming to my sister and myself: 'Look at that man! He'll drive me to my grave. Let him be a warning to you, children!'

(2) So much for what my wife thought fit to say about my family. And, when she talked about my 'first-class education', she was equally wide of the mark. It is true I went to a naval training school. But as I was given no pocket money I could never join the other cadets in their outings, and this made me bitter and morose.

Towards the end we were wretchedly poor, but took care that nobody should know it. For instance, on the days when we had only bread for dinner, my mother always put a row of pots on the fire, so as to give anyone who dropped in the impression we were going to have a copious meal.

I made my wife's acquaintance soon after I left the training school. She always declares it was a case of love at first sight, but that is only her romantic way. Actually there was no romance about it. My wife lived in an out-of-the-way village where her father was the burgomaster, and she wanted to move to a big town like Groningen. As for me, I relished the idea of marrying a girl whose father was a rich and respected man, and who had stayed in a boarding school up to the age of eighteen.

But for her I would have gone to sea. She, however, was set against it. 'I'll never marry a sailor. Sailors are nasty rough men who drink too much and have a girl in every port!'

Though he knew it almost by heart, he took the cutting from his pocket and read it through again before continuing.

(3) Also according to Mrs Popinga, I have been a model husband and a good father for sixteen years. That is as false as all the rest. If I have never been unfaithful to my wife, it is because everything one does in Groningen gets known, and she would have led me an intolerable life.

She would not have made scenes as my mother did. She would have behaved as she always did whenever I bought something she disapproved of or smoked one cigar too many. She merely said, 'Very good,' in a special tone, with a sort of snort. After that she did not speak to me for several days and mooned about the house looking like a martyr. If either of the children asked her what was wrong, she would sigh:

'It's your father! He's so unkind. He doesn't understand me.'

Being of a cheerful disposition, I preferred to avoid such incidents and usually managed to do so, but at the cost of limiting myself during the last sixteen years to one evening a week at the Chess Club and an occasional game of billiards.

As a youngster living with my mother I was always wishing I had enough money to go to theatres and cafés as my friends did, and another of my ambitions was to be well dressed instead of wearing my father's cast-off clothes cut down to my size.

As a married man living in my own house – or, rather, my wife's – I always envied those lucky men who can go out in the evenings without having to say where they are going, who are to be seen with pretty girls on their arms, and can take a train to some exciting place whenever they feel like it.

As to my being a good father, I have the gravest doubts. I never actually disliked my children, and, when they were small, I always praised their looks. But that was only to please 'Mum'; really I thought them hideous brats and I cannot say I greatly changed my mind as they grew up.

There is a legend that my daughter has brains because she speaks so seldom; but I know the true reason, which is that she has nothing to say. Also she is a snob and likes to show off the fine house she lives in to her friends. I once overheard a conversation to this effect:

'What's your father's job, Frida?'

'Oh, he's the manager of de Coster's.'

A downright lie, needless to say. The boy is no better; he has none of the defects of his age, which to my mind augurs ill for his future.

If the theory that I am a good father is based on the fact that I often played games with the children, there is nothing in it; I played games with them to pass the time when I was feeling bored. And I always felt bored when at home. I bought a house not because I really wanted it but because in my young days I envied people with houses of their own. I bought a stove of the same make as one I had seen in the house of the wealthiest man I knew. The same is true of my desk.

But to go into details would take me too far afield. Let me sum up. I don't come of a good family, I have been neither a good husband nor a good father, and if my wife professes to think otherwise that is because she wants to pose as a model wife and mother and all the rest of it.

It was only three. He had ample time in hand and he gazed thoughtfully across the café, in which the atmosphere was steadily thickening as the afternoon advanced.

I see from your paper that Basinger, my cashier at de Coster's, stated as follows:

'Popinga was so devoted to the Firm that he may be said to have identified himself with it; the discovery that it was

insolvent must have been a terrible shock and may well
have affected his brain.'

I assure you, Sir, that statements of this sort make very
painful reading. Suppose that someone were to tell you that
you were doomed to eat nothing but black bread and
Bologna sausage for the rest of your days. Would you not, as
a sensible man, try to convince yourself that these were the
ideal diet! Well, for sixteen years I convinced myself that de
Coster and Son was the most substantial and honourable
firm in Holland.

Then one evening at the Saint George tavern (you will
not follow the allusion, but that has no importance) I
discovered, amongst other things of the same nature, that
Julius de Coster was a crook.

'Crook' is perhaps too strong a word. In reality, de Coster
had always done, though without proclaiming it on the
housetops, everything that I had wished to do. For instance,
he had had a mistress, that young woman Pamela whom
I . . .

I am coming to the point. I will only ask you to note this
fact: that for the first time in my life, looking at my face in
the glass, I asked myself:

'What reason is there for you to go on living as you do!'

What reason indeed! And perhaps you will now put the
same question to yourself, and so will many of your readers.
What reason! None at all. That is the discovery I made
when, for the first time, calmly and logically, I applied my
mind to certain problems which invariably one tackles from
the wrong angle. I saw that I had settled into a groove. The
groove of a trusted employee, of a conventional married man
and father, and I had settled into it simply because others
had decided it should be thus and not otherwise. And
suppose I decided for myself, for a change, and decided it
should be otherwise!

You cannot imagine how simple everything became, once I had come to this decision. No more reason to worry what so-and-so might think, what was forbidden or permitted, proper or improper.

For instance, in the past, even if I was merely going to a neighbouring town for the night, there was all the business of packing up and phoning to book a room at an hotel. But all I had to do the other day was to walk to the station and buy a ticket to Amsterdam, a one-way ticket.

There I looked up Pamela; I had heard so much about her from de Coster and for two years had regarded her as the most attractive woman on earth. Wasn't it only natural I should look her up? She asked me what I wanted, and I explained in quite simple language, the sort I am using in this letter. But, instead of taking it seriously, she went into peals of idiotic, insulting laughter.

I ask you, what could it matter to her, since it was her profession? One man more or less . . . Anyhow, I was determined to see it through. Only next day I learned that I had tied the towel a trifle too tight. Indeed, it took so little to cause her death that one cannot help suspecting she suffered from heart disease.

So here, too, your reporter is mistaken all along the line. You have only to read what he says. That I was acting like a madman when I left Groningen. That people in the train noticed the state I was in, and the steward on the ferry-boat saw something 'abnormal' in my behaviour.

Nobody seems to realize that it was before *this happened I was not in my normal state. In those days, when I was thirsty, I didn't dare to say so, or to drop into a café. And often, at friends' houses, I felt called on, out of politeness, to decline what was offered me to eat, however hungry I might be feeling.*

On railway journeys I had to pretend to read a book or

look out of the window, instead of showing any interest in those around me, and to wear gloves, uncomfortable as they might be – because it's the right thing to do when travelling.

And here is something else your reporter says:

'At this stage the man made one of those slips which are the beginning of the end for criminals; in his excitement he left his attaché-case behind him, in the bedroom of the murdered girl.'

That is sheer nonsense. I made no slip, and I was not excited. I had taken my attaché-case with me by force of habit, and, as I did not need it, had to leave it somewhere. Pamela's bedroom did as well as anywhere else. In any case, on learning of her death I would have written to the police to let them know I was responsible for it.

If you doubt this, I need only remind you that it was I myself who yesterday sent Superintendent Lucas an express letter informing him that I had committed another crime.

The heading in your paper is flattering, I admit, with its intimation that I was out to mock the police. But that, too, is a misstatement. I am not out to mock anybody. Nor am I a lunatic, and, if I used some violence with Mlle Rozier, this was not due to a 'mad frenzy'.

Certainly it is difficult explaining to you why I used force, though in several ways it was a repetition of the Pamela episode. For two whole days I had had Mlle Rozier at my disposal, but for some reason she left me cold. Not till I was alone and started thinking about her did I realize she interested me. I paid her a visit to tell her so. And then, most unreasonably, it was she who turned me down!

What possessed her to do this? And why, under the circumstances, should I have refrained from using a little violence? Not too much, for she is a charming young person, and I should have hated to hurt her badly. Any more than

Pamela. What happened to Pamela was pure bad luck. I was a beginner!

So do you begin to see why I feel so outraged at the articles that have been printed today? I do not intend to write to all the newspapers, for that would be too much work, but I was determined to put the record straight.

So you see I am not crazy, nor the 'homicidal maniac' some people think. I am merely a man who at the age of forty has determined to live as he thinks fit, without bothering about convention or the laws; for I have discovered, if somewhat late in life, that I was the dupe of appearances and the truth is that nobody obeys the law if he can help it.

I have no plans for the moment and cannot say if there will be other incidents for the police to investigate. That will depend on how I feel.

Actually, appearances notwithstanding, I am of a peaceful disposition. If one of these days I come across a girl who seems worthwhile I shall very likely marry her, and nothing more will be heard of me. If, however, I am harassed by the powers-that-be and feel like engaging in a life-and-death conflict with them, there are no lengths to which I shall not go.

I have put up with forty years of boredom. For forty years I lived like the hungry urchin who flattens his nose against a teashop window and watches other people eating cake. Now I have learnt that cakes are always to be had by those who have the guts to take them.

By all means, if it amuses you, go on publishing statements that I am mad. But it will only prove that you, Mr Editor, are suffering from delusions, the same delusions as I had before that evening at the Saint George tavern.

In asking you to publish this letter I do not claim the right of reply due to an injured person; I suspect that such a claim would make you smile. Yet why should you regard it as *absurd? Surely if anyone has a right to insist on publication of his answer to allegations made against him in the Press, it is a man who is fighting for his life!*

In the hope of seeing these lines in print tomorrow, I beg to remain, – Your most obedient servant (untrue of course, it's just a formula), Kees Popinga.

Though his arm was aching, it was a long time since he'd spent such an agreeable hour. So pleasant had it been that he was moved to try his hand at another letter, in a different vein. The station clock pointed to half past four, and the lamps had just been turned on. The waiter found it quite natural that a customer should kill time by disposing of his correspondence.

To the Editor.

This letter was addressed to a paper flaunting a big headline: '*The Madman from Holland.*'

Your sub-editor fancies himself, no doubt, a mighty clever fellow, but he seems more of an adept at coining comic-opera headlines than in serious journalism. Really, I fail to see why he should have dragged in Holland. I have often read in the newspapers of far more sensational 'crimes,' the protagonists of which were true-born Frenchmen.

Let him also reflect that to stigmatize people one cannot understand as 'madmen' is an obvious way out, but a contemptible one.

If this is the manner in which you usually impart news to your readers, I cannot congratulate you. Kees Popinga.

Another one off his chest!

For a moment he dallied with the idea of returning to the Boulevard Saint-Michel, where he would be sure of finding someone to play chess with. But he finally decided it was wiser to abide by his resolve never to show up twice at the same place. Moreover, a newspaper vendor had just come in and was doing the round of the tables, with the evening papers. Kees bought one and started reading:

The arrest of Kees Popinga, the maniac from Holland, may be expected at any moment. Under the energetic supervision of Superintendent Lucas, the nets are tightening round him. For reasons which our readers will appreciate we shall not divulge the steps that are being taken, or information that might put the criminal on his guard.

We are, however, authorized to state that, according to Mlle Rozier, who is making good progress towards recovery, the murderer is not provided with sufficient money to hold out much longer. Also he can be easily identified, as he has certain habits of which he is unable to break himself. More than this we are not allowed to state.

The only danger is that when Popinga realizes he is cornered he may commit another crime. Precautions have, however, been taken in view of this eventuality.

As Superintendent Lucas remarked to us this morning, this type of crime is happily rare amongst us, though it has a certain number of precedents, especially in Germany and England. Such criminal maniacs, usually sexual degenerates, while completely devoid of moral scruples, have often considerable cunning and a coolness which may take in the casual observer but usually leads them to overreach themselves.

Several trails are being followed, and it can only be a matter of days, if not hours. This morning a man whose appearance tallies with Popinga's was, on information given by a lady passenger in a train, taken into custody at one of the Paris railway stations. However, after careful inquiries at Headquarters, it was ascertained that he is a respectable business man from Strasburg, and he has been set at liberty.

There is one circumstance which makes the task of the detective service none the easier; Popinga speaks four languages fluently and can pass for an Englishman or a German if it suits him.

On the other hand, the description of him given by Mlle Rozier, who at first declined to lay a complaint against him, has provided the police with a number of most useful clues. So our readers need feel no alarm; Popinga's criminal career will very soon be terminated.

Strangely enough, he felt more hopeful than otherwise after reading this journalistic effort. He went down to the lavatory for the sole purpose of examining himself in the looking-glass.

He had not lost weight, and indeed looked very fit. He had toyed with the idea of dyeing his hair and growing a beard, but decided against it. The police would expect him to do something of this sort; he would be safer if he made no change in his appearance. His grey suit, too, was a perfectly ordinary one; no need to get another. Still, it might be worthwhile getting a blue overcoat.

He paid for his drinks, posted his letters at the railway station, and went to a reach-me-down shop he had noticed near the Bastille.

'I want a blue overcoat, please. Navy blue.'

As he said this to the man behind the counter, he became conscious of a new danger. He was developing that fatal thing, a habit; the habit of staring at people with a glint of mockery in his eyes, as if he were asking: 'Well, what do you make of me? It's just as well you don't know whom you're serving – the celebrated Popinga, the madman from Holland!'

He tried on a dozen overcoats, all too short or too tight, before one was produced that fitted him more or less. It was in a shoddy material, but he said he would take it.

'Where shall we send your old one, sir?'

'Don't bother to send it. If you'll wrap it up I'll take it with me.'

It was little things like that which were so dangerous. Even to walk the streets wearing a new overcoat and carrying a brown-paper parcel had its perils. Fortunately night had fallen, the Seine was near by, and he could get rid of the incriminating parcel by dropping it in the river.

For all the disgusting nonsense they talked about him, those journalists served one useful purpose anyhow; they gave him clues as to what his opponent, Superintendent Lucas, had in mind. But wait! Wasn't it possible that Lucas had them publish those statements just to throw dust in his eyes?

Really it was quite thrilling! He and the superintendent did not know each other, had never set eyes on each other. But they were matching their wits and intuitions like two chess players playing a game in the dark, unable to see each other's moves.

Why, he wondered, did those fellows writing in the papers think, or profess to think, that he'd commit another crime? Probably, he decided, in the hope of egging him on to doing something rash.

So they thought him open to 'suggestion'! They assumed that, if not actually mad, he had a weak, unbalanced mind, the sort of mind that lets itself be influenced by what others choose to say!

Another problem: what pointers had Jeanne given the police about him? That he dressed in grey? But this was common knowledge. That he smoked cigars? That he was clean-shaven? That he had only three thousand francs on him?

There was nothing serious to worry about in all this. Still, it was vexing being unable to read the superintendent's thoughts. What instructions had he given his men? Where were they making searches, and on what lines?

Perhaps Lucas imagined that Kees would want to be present

when the motor thieves were arrested, and take to prowling round the Juvisy garage.

Not he!

Or that he would go on haunting the Montmartre district.

Wrong again!

Or perhaps Lucas thought he would attempt to get away from Paris, and was having the stations watched.

Though he tried to keep himself from doing so, Kees was beginning to glance over his shoulder now and then, and to halt in front of shops to see if he were being followed. Gazing at a map of Paris posted at the entrance of a Métro station, he fell to wondering in which district he would spend the night. The police would probably make a thorough inspection of the hotels in certain parts of Paris, and check the identity papers of the people staying in them. But which district, or districts, would Lucas pick on?

After all, he wasn't feeling sleepy, so why go to bed at all? On the previous day he had noticed a cinema on one of the Boulevards which had a continuous performance lasting till six in the morning. It was unlikely Lucas would think of looking for him in a cinema.

Anyhow, whatever else he did, he must guard against this habit which was growing on him – of staring at people, especially women, in an ironical way, as if asking:

'Don't you recognize me? Aren't you afraid of me?'

He had caught himself going out of his way to do this. That must be why, though he hadn't realized what prompted him, he always chose restaurants where the service was done by waitresses.

Halting under a streetlamp, he noted in his pocket-book: *'Must be careful how I look at people.'*

One remark especially in the article he had just read was worrying him: the suggestion that he was likely to betray himself. How had they guessed that this was a sort of obsession with him, that it went against the grain to be always a nonentity, one of the common herd, and that often, particularly in dark and lonely streets, he had an impulse to buttonhole the first passerby and ask indignantly:

'Do you mean to say you don't know who I am?'

Still, now he was forewarned, that danger was ruled out. He could train himself to look at people naturally – as if he were really a nonentity and not a public figure.

His thoughts took a new turn. How was Julius de Coster feeling now that he knew about it? For he was sure to know; the English and German papers had plenty to say of Kees's exploits. De Coster, anyhow, would have to admit that he had always had a wrong opinion of his employee. And, when he remembered the way in which he had harangued Kees at the Saint George – like a man of experience talking to a simpleton incapable of understanding him – he must feel pretty small!

For now the employee had eclipsed the employer, beaten him at his own game! There was no getting behind that. Somewhere in London, Berlin, or Hamburg, de Coster was now engaged in the tedious formalities of launching a new concern, handing out all the confidence-inspiring humbug such ventures call for. Whereas he, Popinga, had no need to truckle; he could say bluntly what he thought, to everyone.

One day, if only to discover de Coster's reactions, he must put a Personal in the *Morning Post* as they'd agreed on. Only, how was he to get the answer?

He was still walking; half of his life now consisted of this interminable tramping up and down the streets of Paris, jostled by people who didn't know ... His hand thrust deep in his pockets, he was fingering half-unconsciously the razor, shaving-brush, and toothbrush.

Suddenly he found the solution. As at chess, he'd never fail to find a solution for each new problem as it arose! All he had to do was to pick out an hotel and send two letters to himself, addressed to that hotel, under any name he chose. That would put him in possession of two envelopes addressed to him, and, if he showed these at the post office, he would be able to collect a letter sent to him *poste restante*.

Why not act at once? Once again he turned into a brasserie. He preferred this type of establishment to the true Parisian café, where the customers are wedged together and the tables absurdly small. And the brasseries were more like the beer-houses one sees in Holland.

'The telephone directory, please.'

He opened it at random, chanced on the Rue Brey, a street he did not know, and selected an hotel in it, the Beauséjour.

After that he wrote a letter, or rather slipped a blank sheet into an envelope which he addressed: '*Mr Smithson, Hôtel Beauséjour, 14 rue Brey.*'

Why not have done with the two envelopes now he had started. Writing backhand, he addressed another envelope to '*Mr Smithson.*'

And also why not use the express letter service? Indeed, why not go the whole hog now he was about it and ask for money from de Coster, who probably was shaking in his shoes at the thought that he, Kees, might give him away?

Kees to Julius. Send five thousand Smithson, poste restante, Paris P.O. 42.

These small activities filled the time till eleven at night, for he went about them leisurely and amused himself by writing with especial care, in an elegant copperplate hand.

'Some stamps, waiter.'

After that he went to the telephone box, called up the Hôtel Beauséjour, began by speaking English, and switched over to French with a strong Anglo-Saxon accent.

'Mr Smithson speaking. I shall be coming to the Beauséjour tomorrow. If any mail arrives for me, please keep it.'

'Certainly, sir.'

One up against Superintendent Lucas, who certainly hadn't reckoned on this new, bold move by his opponent!

The voice went on:

'Do you want a room with a bathroom?'

'Of course.'

He was vexed with himself for feeling a slight emotion because it was a woman's voice that had answered on the phone. That was something he must avoid at all costs; the evening paper had made it quite clear that the police were expecting him to assault another woman and thus furnish them with further clues.

'But I shan't do anything of the sort,' he told himself. 'On the contrary, I shall spend a quiet night at the cinema. And tomorrow I shall turn up at the Beauséjour as if I'd just arrived by train.'

Another sign that he was keeping his wits about him was that he called in at a second café, asked for a railway timetable, and ascertained that a train arrived from Strasburg at 5.32.

'I'll say I've come from Strasburg.'

So nothing had been left undone. He was free now to go to the pictures, and it was reassuring to discover that the ushers at this cinema were male.

What could Superintendent Lucas be up to? And Louis, who was certainly back in Paris by now? And Goin? And that girl Rose, whom for no particular reason he thoroughly detested?

9

*The episode of the girl in blue
and the young man with the
crooked nose*

Why couldn't those wretched fellows, the journalists, have
added just a few lines more? Usually they spread themselves,
state and discuss the views the police are taking, the clues that
are being followed up, and even add a lifelike photograph of
the leading sleuth employed on the case.

Kees was struck by the fact that Lucas's photograph hadn't
appeared in any paper. Needless to say, this was of no great
importance. It wasn't to be supposed that the superintendent
in person roamed the streets of Paris in quest of Kees – he left
that to understrappers. Still, Kees regretted that no portrait
had appeared; it might have helped him to take the measure of
his antagonist.

It was not so much the silence of the Press that made him
feel uneasy as his conviction that the newspapers were silent
under orders. For instance, the paper which published Kees's
long letter added only the following lines by way of comment:

> A smile played on the superintendent's face as he read this
> letter, and when he handed it back to us he merely shrugged his
> shoulders.
>
> 'What do you think of it?' we asked.
>
> The superintendent's answer was terse and non-committal.
> 'Priceless!'

Which conveyed absolutely nothing to Popinga. One of the
things he would have particularly liked to learn was whether

that woman he had slept with in an hotel, and whose name he had forgotten to ask, had subsequently realized who he was and made a report to the police.

The importance of this was that, if it was known that he carried a razor and shaving-brush about with him in his pockets, and if, moreover, he persisted in having someone to sleep with him at night, he would soon be identified.

The trouble was that he found it disagreeable sleeping alone. He had tried it at the Beauséjour, where he had duly received the two letters that would enable him to call at the *poste restante* under the name of Smithson.

He had tried it again on the next night at an hotel in the Vaugirard district, and had all but got up in the small hours to scour the streets in quest of a bedfellow. For he had noticed an odd phenomenon. When he had a girl with him he went to sleep at once and had a relatively good night's rest. But when he was by himself he began thinking, gently at first, like a vehicle starting down a gradient, but gradually the thoughts came faster and faster, swarms and swarms of them, and all so painful that he had to turn on the light and sit up in bed to rid his mind of them.

He supposed that, had he mentioned this to anyone, he would have been told that he was suffering from remorse. The absurdity of any such idea was proved by the fact that never once did he think of Pamela, who was dead, whereas Jeanne's form rose constantly before him, and he had hurt her very little, nor indeed would she, on her own initiative, have reported against him to the police. Rose, too, haunted him, surly-faced and hostile, though he had never harmed her. Why of all the phantoms of his mind was it Rose who seemed the most malignant? And why did he keep dreaming that Jeanne, after her green eyes had lingered on him for some moments in a look half humorous, half tender, pressed her lips to his eyelids and laid her cool, slim fingers on his hands?

Wouldn't it be better to have bad nights than risk being spotted by some woman picked up in the street? And was it too much to hope that sooner or later some journalist would be humane, or naïve, enough to make known what steps the police were taking, what places they were watching, and so forth?

Since all his letters, including the express letter to the superintendent, had been written as from brasseries, they would probably keep all establishments of this sort under surveillance. But, even if they neglected to do this, such places were bound to be dangerous, for waiters, if not actually police spies, are professionally observant; they read the papers and, as they go about their work, have ample opportunity to study the faces of their customers.

Why couldn't the papers say frankly:

'Within the last twenty-four hours five or six foreigners who asked for writing materials at cafés were, on information given by the management, taken to the police station and required to prove their identity'?

Meanwhile, as the papers vouchsafed no information, Kees was obliged to take all sorts of perhaps quite needless precautions, and towards nightfall he found that his nerves were getting on edge.

The fact that it was New Year's Eve contributed to this. In most cafés it was impossible to get served, as the staff were busy preparing for the night's festivities, waiters standing on the tables hanging paper festoons and bunches of mistletoe.

It recalled to Kees his experiences on Christmas Eve, a week before, at the *café-tabac* in the Rue de Douai, where Jeanne had come to see him. Wonderful woman! She had actually deserted a cheerful party, with Louis and his friends, to step across the road on two occasions and talk to Kees. And it recalled, too, that mad drive in the stolen car, his first glimpse of the garage, the snowbound railway lines, the night-long rumble of trains and clanking of buffers.

He walked on. During these last few days, owing to his suspicions about café waiters, he had kept on the move almost continuously, and whenever he stopped had chosen humble bars of the type one finds scattered all over Paris and regarding which one wonders how they manage to keep going, for no customers are ever to be seen inside.

He didn't feel like sleeping and fell to wondering how his opponent, Lucas, was spending New Year's Eve. What could be the sort of place a high official of the *Police Judiciaire* would patronize on such occasions?

Kees was rather bored with things this evening, but he knew the feeling would wear off once the festive season with its atmosphere of febrile gaiety was over and one wasn't plagued by the notion that one must amuse oneself at all costs.

Fearing he might be tempted to return to the Rue de Douai to see if the flower-seller was there again, he had deliberately gone to the other end of Paris, to Les Gobelins, which struck him as one of the dreariest districts he had so far explored. There were long, dingy avenues, neither old nor modern, rows of barrack-like houses, and the restaurants were full of people neither rich nor poor.

Finally he drifted into one such restaurant, at the corner of a street; it offered a four-course supper, champagne included, for forty francs.

'By yourself?' The waiter seemed surprised.

Not only was he alone, but he was one of the first to enter, and this gave him time to take stock of his surroundings. He watched the five members of the band strolling in one by one and chatting with each other as they tuned their instruments, and waiters placing sprays of mistletoe beside the plates and folding napkins fanwise as at small-town wedding banquets.

Then the customers began to arrive, and it was more and more like a wedding banquet; so much so indeed that Kees felt half inclined to make a move.

For all these people seemed to know each other, and tables were being run together so that large groups could sup in company. There were only families here, families like those he had seen in the boxes at the Cinéma Saint-Paul, local tradespeople no doubt, the men well washed, faintly redolent of scent and wearing their best clothes, the women almost without exception in blatantly new dresses.

Within less than a quarter of an hour the restaurant, which when Kees entered had been funereally calm, had become full of noise, a hubbub of voices, the chink of glasses, clatter of knives and forks. These people had come here with the intention of having a good time, and with one accord were going to it, the middle-aged women, especially the stout ones, setting the pace.

Kees worked his way through the forty-franc supper without thinking overmuch. For some reason or other, his surroundings brought back to his mind that dinner party at the Professor's house when he had put sugar in the oxtail soup. At one moment he caught himself wondering again why everyone seemed to expect him to commit another crime *à la Paméla*.

He had a corner place. At a long table near by, several families who knew each other had joined forces. They were presided over by a prosperous-looking middle-aged man with a black moustache so sleek that it seemed varnished. He wore a dinner jacket that was too tight for him and a gold albert slung across his waistcoat. His self-important air led Kees to surmise he was a town councillor or something of the sort.

His wife was no less impressive, a buxom matron in a closely fitting black silk dress, so lavishly bedecked with diamonds – or paste? – that her chest looked like a jeweller's show-case.

On the left of the man was their daughter, who took after both her parents, yet was almost pretty. One day, no doubt, she would resemble her mother, but meanwhile she had the freshness of youth and a pink-and-white complexion that went well with her pale blue dress. She was already inclined to plumpness, and her bodice was so tight that sometimes she seemed to have trouble in breathing.

What could these people matter to Kees? As he ate, he listened absentmindedly to the band, and when people started dancing between the courses it never occurred to him that he might join in.

However, that was precisely what happened – and in a really idiotic way. Just as the band was striking up a waltz, he happened to glance towards the girl in blue. Evidently she took his glance for an invitation, for she responded with a smile and a slight movement indicating she was willing to dance with him.

Then she rose, patted her skirt to get the creases out, went up to Kees, and a moment later they had joined the dancing couples. The girl had clammy hands, and there came from her a stale yet not unpleasing odour. She leant with all her weight on her partner, pressing her chest to his. Her parents watched with approval.

Catching sight of himself in a mirror, Kees could hardly believe it was he in this absurd position, with his arm round the waist of a plump, amiable young person. Indeed, he was unable to repress a sardonic grin. What a shock it would be for her if he told her that –

An infernal din broke out from the drums and cymbals; the band had stopped playing in the middle of a bar and everyone was shouting, laughing, kissing. Kees saw the pink face draw close to his, and felt two soft, moist kisses, one on each cheek.

The New Year had begun. People were going up to each other, slapping each other on the back, mock-fighting. Kees, who felt rather at a loss, had more kisses bestowed on him by the girl's mother, then by a fat lady at their table, who looked like a greengrocer. Paper streamers whizzed out in all directions and the air grew thick with pellets of coloured cotton wool that the waiters had hastily distributed round the tables.

Then the band started playing again, and, though he had given no sign to her, Kees found the girl in blue once more at his side.

'Don't look to your left,' she whispered in his ear as they began dancing. 'I don't know what he'll do. And please keep to the right of the room. I'm so frightened he may make a scene.'

'Who?'

'Don't look! He'd guess we were talking about him. You'll see him in a moment. A young man in a dinner jacket, by himself – with brown hair parted on the side. We were practically engaged, but I turned him down as I'd heard some nasty things against him.'

Perhaps the two or three glasses of champagne she had drunk had gone to her head. In any case, expansiveness was, so to speak, in the air; decorum at a discount. Hadn't they all just exchanged kisses? Many indeed were still doing so, hunting up people at remote tables who'd been left out, dragging girls under the mistletoe, laughing and screeching with delight.

'I thought I'd better let you know,' the girl went on. 'You understand, don't you?'

Kees wasn't sure if he did, but he said, 'Yes.'

'Perhaps you'd better not dance with me again. I know the sort he is, he wouldn't stick at anything. In fact, he swore to me I'd never be another man's sweetheart.'

Fortunately the dance ended just then and the girl went back to her place, while her mother gave Kees a discreet smile as if to thank him on behalf of the family.

From his corner Kees glanced across the room and at once spotted the man the girl had spoken of. Not only was he the only man with his hair parted on the side, but he had a crooked nose, which made him still more conspicuous.

It was easy to see that he was in a rage. His face was white, his lips were trembling, and he kept on shooting furious glances at the girl in blue.

Why did the scene bring to Kees's mind an amateurishly painted picture with all the facial peculiarities of the characters grotesquely overdone? In the garish light everything showed up in sharp relief, and the band, if small in numbers, made up for this by the infernal racket with which they filled the room. Anything was enough to send people into fits of semi-hysterical laughter – a paper streamer caught in a girl's hair, a coloured pellet landing on a man's neck or nose. Everyone seemed infected with a delirious, almost subhuman frenzy of merriment, with the exception of the young man with the crooked nose, who was scowling like a melodrama villain.

It struck Kees he would have done better to drink the cheap champagne provided, as everyone else had done. In that case, he might have felt more in harmony with them, and it would have been amusing to see the New Year in, in this atmosphere of homely, unsophisticated revelry.

Now and again the girl gave him an understanding look, that said:

'You're quite right. Better not ask me to dance again. You can see for yourself the state he's in!'

Who could he be, this young man in a temper? A bank clerk? More likely a draper's assistant, judging by his special brand of elegance. In any case, a passionate young fellow who fancied himself the hero of a thriller or the protagonist of a romantic play, with the town councillor's fair daughter as his opposite number.

That worthy gentleman danced with his wife, then with his daughter, then in turn with all the ladies at their table, bobbing up and down, indulging in all sorts of pranks, playing to the gallery, wearing a fireman's helmet made of coloured paper.

Paper caps had been distributed, and Kees's was a naval

officer's cap with a white top, but he'd taken good care not to wear it.

Twice the girl's mother gave him an inviting smile, that said:

'Won't you dance again?'

And undoubtedly she had whispered in her husband's ear:

'He's a real gentleman, I'm sure!'

Meanwhile a young man whom Kees hadn't noticed before had started dancing with the girl in blue. Quite suddenly it dawned on him that the danger she had spoken of wasn't mere imagination; that the man with the crooked nose really meant business!

On ten occasions during the dance, he seemed on the point of getting up, and Kees noticed with disquiet that he had his right hand permanently in his pocket.

'Waiter!' he shouted.

'Yes, sir?'

He had just had an intuition. Something was going to happen within the next five minutes, and the sooner he got away the better. The others were too busy amusing themselves to notice, but for him it was as if already the man with the crooked nose had made some fateful move.

'Well, where's the bill?'

'Surely you're not thinking of leaving already, sir? It isn't one yet.'

'How much do I owe you?'

'You really want to go? Let's see. Forty plus eight plus seven . . . fifty-five francs.'

Kees's apprehensions were developing into panic. Every second added to his peril, and he fretted with impatience as he waited for his overcoat to be brought from the cloakroom, his eyes fixed on the 'villain' who was beginning to edge his way forward, while the girl in blue went on dancing and now and again bestowed a smile on Kees.

'Thanks.' He rose so abruptly as nearly to upset the table.

The town councillor's wife gave him a reproachful glance that said: 'Going already? And you haven't asked me to dance once!'

His hat still in his hand, he pushed his way to the revolving door.

When he was halfway round, the shot rang out, distinctly audible in spite of the noise of the band. It was followed by an appalled silence. Kees was tempted to look back, but realized the least delay might be disastrous. He was in imminent danger: on no account must he be involved in the aftermath of a *crime passionnel*.

He turned left, then right, without the least idea where he was going, and walking as quickly as he dared. Was the girl dead? he wondered, and pictured her stretched on the floor like a big golden-haired doll, amongst the coloured pellets and paper streamers.

He had covered half a mile when he saw a police car travelling full-speed in the opposite direction. A quarter of an hour later he suddenly found he was in the Boulevard Saint-Michel; on his left was the café where he had played chess. He halted to take breath, and only then did he wholly realize the danger he had run. His knees began to knock together, and a cold sweat broke out on his forehead.

How idiotic it would have been, when he was pitting himself against Superintendent Lucas, the Press, and indeed the world at large, to let himself get caught just because a jealous shop-boy let off a revolver! Anyhow, he'd learnt his lesson; for the future he must steer clear of crowds, for in a crowd things are apt to happen – crimes and accidents – and in such cases the police are sure to check identity papers.

Nor must he linger in the Latin Quarter. Rightly or wrongly, he was convinced that this was one of the places where they were looking for him. Similarly, Montmartre and Montparnasse were ruled out. It would be safest to move to some quieter district, like Les Gobelins, find a small hotel, and go to bed.

Moreover, he had work to do; he hadn't written up his diary during the last twenty-four hours. Not that there was anything much to record, except that revolver shot.

But he had come to a new decision. Since anything might happen to him, and the notebook as it stood wasn't enough to make people understand, he had resolved to spend his leisure time in compiling nothing short of a full-dress autobiography.

The idea had been suggested by a heading in the newspaper which had published his letter:

Strange Revelations by a Murderer.

The letter was followed by some lines of comment.

As our readers will observe, we have been enabled to present to them a human document of the highest interest. Indeed, the annals of crime have few such documents to show.

Is Popinga telling the truth or playing a part? Or deceiving himself? As for deciding whether he is sane or otherwise, we own our incompetence.

For this reason we have submitted this letter to two of our most eminent psychiatrists, and we hope to be able to publish their opinions tomorrow, in the belief that this will not only interest our readers but be of assistance to the police.

Kees had read his letter twice over, and felt dissatisfied with it now that he saw it in print. Somehow it didn't produce the same effect as when he had seen it on the brasserie notepaper. Several points were explained, some left wholly unexplained. Indeed, he had half a mind to write to the psychiatrists and ask them to defer forming opinions at this stage.

For instance, his remarks about his father might easily lead people to believe that, as a drunkard's son, he was a victim of heredity; whereas actually his father hadn't taken to excessive drinking until some years after his son was born. Nor had he clearly explained that, though he had been something of a recluse from his schooldays onward, this was because he felt that people did not accord him the place to which he was entitled.

Yes, he would have to start all over again, beginning from his early childhood. He would have to point out, amongst other things, that he could easily have excelled in any sphere of action – which was indeed the truth. As a schoolboy he had always been the best at games. When he saw another boy performing some athletic feat, he never failed to say:

'It's quite easy, really!'

And, without any preparation, right away, he'd bring it off, at his first shot.

But it was regarding his family life that people would go most astray. He could see now that he'd failed to present it as it really was. For example, he would certainly be accused of lack of affection for his wife and children. Nothing could be wider of the mark. He was really fond of them; that was the correct phrase. In other words, he always did his duty by them, was what is called 'a good father', and no one could say a word against him on this score.

Looking back, he saw that he had always tried his very best to be a man like other men, respectable, good-mannered, honourable, and on the whole he had succeeded. His children had been well fed, well dressed, and comfortably housed. Each had a separate bedroom, and they shared a bathroom between them; not many parents did their children as well as that. Nor did he ever grudge money for household expenses. What more could anyone expect of him?

Still, one could do all that and feel out of it all the same; have an obscure sense that it wasn't enough to fill a life and that one could have done so much better.

That was what he must make clear. How, for instance, in the evenings when Frida – how queer it was now even to murmur her name! – was poring over her lessons, Mum sticking pictures into her album, and he sat in an armchair, fiddling with the knobs of the wireless while puffing on a cigar, somehow he couldn't help feeling rather lost, out of tune with his surroundings. What wonder if he had a curious thrill whenever he heard the whistle of a passing train, three hundred yards from his house!

He walked on and on, up dark byways, along brilliantly lighted streets. Sometimes he encountered bands of revellers with paper caps on like the town councillor, capering and shouting, arm in arm.

And there were others, solitary men who walked slowly, picking up cigarette-ends from the gutters, and halting outside the cafés in a vague hope of something turning up. He walked past uniformed policemen spending their New Year's Eve on duty at street corners, keeping perfunctory watch upon the cheerful crowd. How perfunctory was evidenced by the fact that not one of them had a good look at Kees's face.

Yes, he would write his memoirs; indeed, he'd already tried to make a start that morning, but failed. That was because he was alone at the time, in an hotel bedroom.

When he was alone all the ideas went out of his head – or, rather, changed out of recognition – and he was seized by a desire to go and look at himself in the glass to see if his face, too, had changed.

It would be better to write in a brasserie, where the air throbbed with the heat from a stove and was laden with odours of humanity. The trouble was that if he asked a waiter to bring notepaper the man might quite likely turn suspicious, run to the phone and call the police.

When all was said and done, what freedom of action still remained to him? He had only the vaguest idea, since that damned fellow Lucas gave nothing away and enjoined silence on the newspapers.

There was no question of taking a train. If anything was certain, it was certain that in every station there was a detective with a full description of Kees's appearance, on the watch.

He hadn't yet made up his mind whether to sleep alone or not. He knew it was dangerous getting a woman of the street to spend the night with him, but he'd have to risk it. Otherwise it meant an almost sleepless night, and he would wake up feeling mentally and physically below par – which was more dangerous still.

What he really needed was some woman like Jeanne, who would have understood and even helped him; for she had brains enough for that. Moreover, he felt sure she'd realized the sort of man he was, very different from that wretched gigolo Louis, who was only good for stealing cars and selling them in the provinces – a form of crime which called for no special skill. Hadn't he, Popinga, brought it off at his first attempt, without turning a hair?

He wondered if the police had taken his advice and were watching the Juvisy garage. If he had given that advice, it wasn't merely out of spite. Once Louis was in jail, with Goin and the others, Jeanne would be alone, and then . . .

Meanwhile he had to sleep somewhere; the problem of where to sleep, recurring as it did each night, was becoming ever more acute. Kees had no idea where he was. Only after he had examined the names of two streets and that of a Métro station did he discover that he was in the Boulevard Pasteur. He hadn't been in this part of Paris before, and it seemed to him as depressing as the Gobelins district.

Lights were still on in some of the flats, and people who had been to parties were leaving by the street doors and hunting round for taxis. A man and woman brushed past him and he heard the woman say:

'Really, I think you needn't have danced with her so often, considering it's New Year's Day.'

A queer life! A queer night! An old tramp was sleeping, stretched full length, on a wooden bench. Two policemen were pacing up and down, chatting of their private affairs, about their pay most likely.

It was painful for Kees to have to resign himself to sleeping alone, and especially hard tonight as . . . How absurd! At the time he hadn't noticed anything, but now it was over, he found that the memory of the girl in blue, whom he had held in his arms, set his senses tingling. And of course he had got accustomed to the rather squalid, happy-go-lucky intimacy that comes of spending each night with a woman one had never seen before.

Why not risk it just once again? Only there were no solitary women about – even in front of the smaller hotels, their usual beat, none was to be seen. Did those women, too, celebrate the New Year by a night off?

Walking on, he caught sight of Montparnasse Station and, judging this a danger spot, gave it a wide berth.

Half an hour later he had still found no bedfellow. But he was too tired to go on searching. In a thoroughly bad temper he rang the doorbell of an hotel; there was always the chance a chambermaid might show him to his room. But he was greeted by an old night porter, as surly as himself, who, as Kees had no luggage, insisted on payment in advance.

As ill luck would have it, Kees's watch had stopped and he had no idea of the time when at last he went to sleep, or when he rose. The window of his room gave on a courtyard and he was unable to judge the hour by the noises in the street.

Only when he was outside did he realize how early it was; everything was quiet and the streets had that dreary morning-after air that follows festive nights. The only people about were a few suburbanites in their best clothes, who had come by early trains to present New Year's greetings to relatives or friends. To make things worse, the sky was grey and the streets were swept by an icy wind.

The one bright spot was that in today's paper there would be the opinions of the two psychiatrists. As he walked down a street leading to the École Militaire he unfurled a newspaper and started reading.

> Professor Abram, who was good enough to receive our representative, holidays notwithstanding, could only give Popinga's letter a hasty perusal. Pending a closer study of its contents, he gave us the benefit of his first impressions. He believes the Dutchman to be a paranoiac who may become extremely dangerous if deeply wounded in his self-esteem; all the more dangerous as persons of this type keep remarkably cool under all circumstances and cannot be recognized for what they are except by experts.
>
> Professor Linze, who is away from Paris and will not be back for two days, will give us his opinion on his return.
>
> The police have nothing new to communicate. Superintendent Lucas was busy all day yesterday investigating the activities of a gang of dope-traffickers, but his colleagues have been following up the Popinga case, and we understand that a new element is about to enter into it, though as to this the strictest secrecy is being observed at Headquarters.
>
> All that we are able to say is that it seems Popinga will not remain at large very much longer.

'Why?' He said it aloud. Yes, why shouldn't he remain at large? And why this lack of details? And why call him a 'paranoiac'?

He had seen the word before and had a vague notion of what it meant. A pity the newspaper hadn't explained it, for the benefit of its readers! If only he could have access to a dictionary! At Groningen one had to sign in a register when consulting a book in the Public Library. Probably it was the same at Paris. And though one finds the telephone directory and railway timetables in cafés, dictionaries are not provided.

It was positively disgusting! From the turn things were taking it seemed as if there were a general conspiracy against him. That reference, for instance, to a 'new element' in the case, and the mystery they made about it, looked like malice prepense.

And hadn't Jeanne, who ought to know, said that Lucas was a swine? Kees was coming back to his first opinion, that the detective was lying low deliberately, waiting for his victim to blunder into his net. Certainly all that appeared in the Press about his methods, and the few cryptic remarks he deigned to let fall, pointed to this conclusion.

Well, if that was what Lucas was waiting for, he'd be disappointed; he, Kees, would not let himself be trapped so tamely. His brains were, to say the least of them, a match for the superintendent's – not to mention those of the mental specialist who could do no better than, like the pompous ass he was, fall back on a word like 'paranoiac'.

As others had said 'homicidal maniac,' or 'sadist'. As that woman at the Montmartre hotel had said he was 'a melancholy sort', and the thin girl had decided he 'liked them plump'!

He had this advantage over them all; he, anyhow, knew what he was.

He read the article again – it was far too short for his liking – as he sipped a cup of coffee and ate a croissant in a small tavern with tiled walls in turn-of-the-century style. A memory of the girl in blue came to his mind, and he turned to the police news in the paper.

> Last night, while the New Year's Eve festivities were in progress in a restaurant in the Gobelins district, a jilted lover, Jean R . . ., fired a revolver-shot at Germaine H., the daughter of a

wine-merchant who is one of our most esteemed town council-lors. Fortunately the shot went wide and only slightly wounded a young man, Henri V . . ., who, after medical attention, was able to return to his home. Jean R . . . was arrested and is still in custody.

He couldn't help smiling to himself. The tragedy would prob-ably have a happy ending. For he strongly suspected that Ger-maine H., as she was called, had acted as she did deliberately.

The next thing was to discover if his Personal in the *Morning Post* had borne fruit – assuming that de Coster hadn't omitted to read the paper daily. The post office to which the *poste restante* letter was to be addressed was halfway across Paris, and Kees travelled there by bus. He went to the counter and displayed the envelopes addressed to 'Mr Smithson'.

The clerk rummaged in the pigeonhole marked 'S' and gave him a letter, the address on which was typed. He retreated to a corner to open it. It contained four pound-notes and a sheet of paper with a few lines, also in typescript.

> Sorry to send so little, but it's all I can manage for the moment. A fresh start is always uphill work. Keep in touch, however, and you can count on my doing my utmost.

That was all. Really, it looked as if de Coster wasn't at all surprised by what Kees had done. In fact, nobody seemed surprised. All they did was to write him down as 'paranoiac'! Of course, Mum was nearly as bad with her 'amnesia'!

10

How Kees Popinga changed his shirt,
and the police and Chance conspired
to hit him below the belt

He wasn't losing heart, of course; that would have been doing too good a turn to those fine fellows of the Press and the police. Still, whenever he opened a newspaper, or even saw one on sale, he couldn't help smiling rather ruefully.

For nobody seemed to realize his position, that he was fighting against odds, playing the game courageously; nor that certain details of daily life can be extraordinarily vexatious for one in his position.

Thus, the first time he had changed his shirt, in a café lavatory – lavatories played an important part in his nomadic life – he had walked out into the street with the soiled shirt under his arm and disposed of it in an outside urinal. It was a near thing he wasn't caught. A policeman had noticed him, and as Kees walked away, came up to see what he'd got rid of. And Kees had had to make a bolt for it!

Now that for the second time he was changing into a new shirt, he proposed to drop the old one in the Seine. But it's far from being as easy as it sounds, to find a lonely place on the river bank. Always at the last moment one catches sight of a fisherman, a tramp, a courting couple, or a lady taking her dog for a walk.

Who had the faintest notion of all these tiresome complications he had to cope with? Certainly not the Pressmen. He had supplied them not only with a 'story' to their hearts' desire, but with columns of free copy. But not one of them had shown a spark of gratitude, or even common humanity!

Of course he didn't expect them to say they wished him luck in his match against the authorities; nor to devote two front-page columns to him daily. But he knew what he meant; in handling cases of this sort the Press can present the facts in such a way as to enlist public sympathy for the 'criminal' – which was, in fact, the line they usually took in France – or, alternatively, they can make him appear odious.

Why had they chosen the second course in writing about Kees? Was he to see the hand of Lucas in this departure from their usual practice?

He had robbed no one; that should reassure the bourgeois element. True, Pamela had died; but he hadn't intended to kill her. And in both his exploits the 'victims' were women of easy virtue – which was enough to allay the fears of all respectable women.

With a host of crimes on his conscience, Landru, who was ugly as sin into the bargain, had had half the public on his side. Why then should the newspapers be down on him, Popinga, and, when not relegating him to silence, publish such futilities as:

> Dr Linze, whose views on the Popinga case we had hoped to set before our readers today, informs us that, much as he would like to accede to our request, he does not feel justified in voicing an opinion on so grave a case, on the strength of a single letter.

So they had come to this, to trivial comments on side-issues, the palterings of psychoanalysts, when what was at stake was his life and liberty! On the following day Professor Abram, who evidently took his colleague's reticence for an aspersion on himself, thought fit to publish a letter in his best heavy-footed style:

I regret to find that a statement I did not make has been attributed to me and, though the affair it concerns is of small importance, I must request you to publish this letter in your columns. In the course of conversation I may have let fall a remark to the effect that I believed Popinga to be suffering from a common form of paranoia; but the weight of a considered diagnosis should not be ascribed to a mere *obiter dictum*.

So, it seemed, even the mental specialists were letting him drop! Even Saladin, the journalist who had written the best articles about him at the start, was drying up, merely publishing brief items without signing them. Kees knew nothing whatever about the man, but he felt this falling-off as bitterly as if a friend had let him down.

And what point was there in publishing such tedious information as:

The accountants who, Christmas notwithstanding, have been hard at work examining the books of Messrs Julius de Coster en Zoon, have notified the authorities that they will require several weeks more to complete their task. Indeed, there are indications that this affair has wider ramifications than was suspected, that it involves more than a financial collapse of the first magnitude, and that a series of deliberate frauds, carried out under the aegis of an honourable name, will be brought to light.

We also learn that, though the Wilhelmina Canal has been dragged repeatedly, de Coster's body has not been found. It is now thought that this was a bogus suicide and that the man has fled to some foreign country.

What earthly interest had this rigmarole for Kees? On the other hand, they made a point of printing – just to tantalize him, maybe – such news items as this:

Superintendent Lucas left for Lyons yesterday. He acknowledged that he was going there for an inquiry, but declined to state whether it concerned the Popinga case or the activities of the gang of dope-runners, some of whom have already been arrested.

Why to Lyons? And why keep harping on a dope-case that nobody was interested in? More aggravating still, why did all this give an impression of a hidden hand at work, a deliberate attempt to throw dust in his eyes?

If there was a hidden hand it could only be the superintendent's. It was he who was making the reporters toe the line. For usually each newspaper conducts its own investigation, has a pet theory, follows up clues, and publishes all it can elicit.

In the Popinga case the obvious step was to interview Jeanne Rozier. But not a single journalist had anything to say about her; it was even impossible to know if she had recovered and resumed her 'work' at Picratts. Nor was there a word about Louis; it was not even said whether he had returned from Marseilles.

Really, there was something underhand about the whole proceedings, not a vestige of fair play. Surely by now someone had reported to the police that he, or she, had come in contact with Kees. That being so, why not mention it in the newspapers?

The answer was obvious. They wanted to put him off his guard, perhaps even to goad him into some indiscretion. Kees shrugged his shoulders and gave a little scornful snort. He wasn't to be caught as easily as that!

All the same, he kept a more careful watch on himself. As he walked the streets he refrained from casting sardonic or inquiring glances at passersby. And he slept by himself, even though it meant a bad night, with long spells of wakefulness and sometimes palpitations of the heart.

An experiment he had tried had warned him of a new danger.

Chance had brought him to the Javel district, one of the slumm-
iest of Paris, and, thinking it a good plan to vary the class of
hotel he stayed in, he had spent the night in a really sordid
one. An error of judgement! He realized that in such a place
his clothes made him conspicuous; these people wondered
what such a 'toff' was doing in their midst.

He must steer a middle course as far as hotels were concerned. In any case, luxury hotels were ruled out; he had now
only twelve hundred francs in hand. One of these days he
would really have to set about making some money. The need
was not immediate, but he might as well start thinking about
it now.

It was the night of 7 January that he had spent in the slums,
and, after dropping his dirty shirt into the Seine, Kees thought
it best to move to another part of Paris before settling down to
read the morning papers. It was raining. For other people that
was a minor infliction. But for him, who had to spend most of
the day in the streets and had no change of clothes, it was a
real hardship. Was it not enough to have every man's hand
against him, but nature must turn nasty too!

He found a comfortable brasserie near the Madeleine, and
almost burst out laughing when his eyes fell on a heading in
the paper to which Saladin contributed:

Motor-thief released by the Police.

The funniest thing was that for several days he had been
expecting something of this sort. He had not been mistaken in
suspecting that some dirty work was going on behind the
scenes. All the same . . .

Yesterday at five we chanced to witness the release of one of
the gang of car thieves arrested last week. The man in question,
who is known as 'Louis', was just leaving Superintendent
Lucas's office. We did our best to ascertain from official sources

why he had been set at liberty, but silence was the order of the day at headquarters.

However, as the result of personal inquiries, we have formed a theory as to the motive for this remarkable release, and have pleasure in communicating it to our readers.

Let it be noted first of all that no Press announcement was made the night of 1/2 January, when Superintendent Lucas, who would not normally be involved in cases of this ilk, presided personally at the arrest of a gang of car thieves.

Why this secrecy? And why has nothing transpired of this important case (of great interest to all car owners in the metropolis), in connection with which no less than four men and one woman have been arrested?

We believe these questions may be answered if we consider the identity of the leader of the gang, known as the Juvisy gang because the cars they stole were camouflaged at a garage at Juvisy before being driven away for sale in the provinces.

This man 'Louis', formerly a drug-trafficker, is Mlle Jeanne Rozier's 'fancy man'. As for Mlle Rozier, our readers will remember . . .

Kees could have made a far better job than his friend Saladin of the rest of the article. And never had his smile held such profound contempt for the Press, for Lucas, for the entire human race. The concluding paragraphs ran:

This explains the personal intervention of Superintendent Lucas in the case. After the arrest of the gang, among them one Rose, a former chamber maid in a house of ill repute and the sister of Goin, the garage-owner, the Press were not informed until Police interrogations were well advanced.

Are we to infer from the fact that Louis has been set at liberty that there is no case against him? Such is not our impression. As no information was forthcoming from headquarters we got in touch with members of the world of gangsterdom, who know Louis well and are knowledgeable in such matters.

'If Louis has been let out,' one of them told us, 'that's because he's been given a job to do, you understand?'

This is borne out by the fact that Louis was seen last night visiting certain bars and giving mysterious instructions to other men of his stamp.

It looks as if from now on Kees Popinga, Mlle Rozier's assailant, is not only being tracked down by the police, but the underworld is on his trail as well. We may therefore assume that his arrest will take place in the very near future, barring some unforeseen development.

At this moment Kees caught sight of himself in a mirror opposite, and noticed that his cheeks were very pale, his lips incapable of conjuring up a smile, however cynical.

His worst fears were being confirmed, and but for Saladin, towards whom he felt much less ill disposed, he would have risked it and gone on moving freely about Paris in ignorance of the plot that had been hatched against him.

Now it was all as clear as daylight. The raid on the garage had been successful, and the gang arrested. Lucas, however, instead of proclaiming it on the housetops, had fooled the public with stories of dope-traffickers. Meanwhile, he had shown Louis the letter in which Kees informed against him, and, as Saladin had pointed out, had struck a treacherous bargain with him.

So that was how things stood! The police were hand-in-glove with Louis, who had been given his liberty so as to track Kees down. But what a confession of weakness! The police unable to carry out their duties without assistance from a criminal!

What Kees felt was more than scorn and indignation; it was profound disgust. He asked for notepaper and got out his fountain-pen, but, when about to start a letter, gave way to a feeling of despair. To whom could he write? To Saladin –

merely to confirm the theory he had advanced? To Lucas – to convey ironical congratulations? To whom, then – and anyhow what use was it?

Now that Louis was on the warpath, they assumed it was all over bar the shouting! From now on, every street-girl, all the denizens of the underworld, owners of shady bars and cheap hotels, would be on the watch, ready to call in the police at the least sign of him.

Though the police had never set eyes on him, Louis had . . .

'Waiter, how much do I owe you?'

He paid, but remained where he was, suddenly conscious of the accumulated weariness of endless hours spent tramping the streets of Paris. Leaning back on the imitation leather upholstery, he gazed dully at the street, black ranks of wet umbrellas jogging past the windows.

So that was how these representatives of law and order looked at it! They had less indulgence for him than for a car thief, an old offender; one, moreover, who made money out of prostitutes. It was impossible to blank the facts. Quite likely, if Louis was successful, they would shut their eyes to the crimes of the Juvisy gang.

'Waiter!'

He felt thirsty. Why not have a glass of brandy? It would help him to think, and there was much thinking to be done.

The truth was, he shouldn't have stopped after that business with Jeanne. He could see it all so clearly now. For he was beginning to understand how public opinion functions. There should have been something more in the newspapers, the very next morning: 'Girl assaulted in a train. Popinga still at large.'

And so on, with some new sensation every day to keep the public thrilled – till he'd become a legendary figure. Would people have been so excited over Landru's fate if he'd killed only one or two women?

Perhaps he had been wrong to write exactly what he thought, instead of lying. Suppose, for instance, he had given them to understand that even in Groningen, where he'd passed for a model of propriety, he had been leading a double life, indulging in all sorts of lurid adventures?

Reading Saladin's article again, he found his first impression confirmed; it was on Louis now, not on himself, Popinga, that the spotlight of publicity was directed; Louis who was being cast for the hero's part! Everybody would be thrilled by the dramatic situation – a criminal, with the connivance of the police, sleuthing a murderer in the Parisian underworld.

Downhearted he refused to be, would never be, whatever happened. But surely he had a right to give way for a moment to fatigue, and to muse on the gross unfairness of it all. How many were after him at this very moment? Hundreds, perhaps thousands of people.

Still, this did not prevent him from enjoying his brandy and gazing idly at the falling rain. Let them look for him; let them peer into the face of every passerby. One man can always beat the mob, provided he keeps his nerve. And he, Popinga, would keep his, in any event.

He had made only one mistake; that of not having from the start treated the whole world as enemies. With the result that no one took him seriously. No one feared him. Almost he was regarded as that semi-comic figure, the lunatic at large. A 'paranoiac', whatever that might be.

Well, they could regard him as they chose. It didn't prevent him from defying Paris, police and populace alike, as he sat in a warm, cosy lounge, sipping his second glass of brandy. Nor would it prevent him from doing whatever he chose to do, something he was going to decide on presently, something that would make them shake in their shoes, every damned one of them, including, the car-thieves, the street-girls, Louis and his gangster friends!

What was it to be? He had plenty of time to think it out; or perhaps the best thing would be to wait for an inspiration, and meanwhile go on watching the crowds streaming past the windows like a flock of foolish sheep. Some were running – as though that got them any forrader! Out in the street stood a caped policeman, looking very pleased with himself as he controlled the traffic with his slim white truncheon and blasts of his whistle. What a dolt the fellow was! If he had any gumption, why, instead of gesticulating like an orchestra conductor in the street, didn't he walk into the brasserie and ask Kees for his identity papers?

That would have settled it. The Popinga case would be closed; Louis and his gang would fade out of the picture, and so would Superintendent Lucas, who, Kees felt sure, believed himself endowed with an extraordinary flair. On that score, surely Kees could give him points; hadn't he sensed what was coming several days in advance and, irksome though it was, slept by himself every night?

A new idea occurred to him. Why not give up sleeping alone from now on? He could always make sure his companion didn't blab!

He felt a rush of blood to his head. As he inspected himself again in the glass, he wondered if he'd really had the idea that had just come to him. Yet, after all, why not? What was there to hinder him?

He looked round. Someone had just addressed him in English; a man who had been writing at a neighbouring table for some minutes.

'Excuse me, sir,' he said amiably. 'Do you by any chance speak English?'

'Yes.'

'You're an Englishman, eh?'

'Yes.'

'In that case, I hope you won't mind my asking your

assistance. I'm an American, and this is my first trip to Paris.
I've been trying to get that waiter to say what stamp I should
put on this letter, and I don't seem able to make him understand.'

Kees called the waiter, translated, and kept his eyes fixed on
the American, who thanked him profusely as he stamped a
letter addressed to New Orleans.

'You're lucky to speak French like that,' he sighed as he
closed the blotter. 'I've been having a lousy time ever since I
got here. Can't even make folks understand when I ask the
way. You know Paris, I suppose?'

'A bit.' It amused Kees to reflect that within a week he'd
explored practically the whole of Paris.

'A good friend of mine gave me the address of a bar that's
run by an American. Pretty near the whole American colony
meets there evenings, so he told me.'

The man had grey hair, a blotchy complexion, a scarlet nose
that confessed his ruling passion.

'It's quite near the Opera,' he continued, 'but I searched for
a half hour and couldn't find it. He took a slip of paper from a
pocket of his capacious overcoat. 'Know where that is? Rue –
how do you say it? – de la Michodière.'

'Yes, I know it.'

'Is it far?'

'Five minutes' walk.'

The man seemed to hesitate, then said:

'I suppose you don't feel like coming round there for a drink?
I've had nobody to talk to for the last two days and I'm feeling
sort of lonesome.'

And Kees? Hadn't he been in a like case for a whole week?

Five minutes later the two men were strolling down the
boulevard. Hearing them talking English, a seedy-looking man
rustled up with a packet of transparent postcards.

'What's he want?' the American asked.

Kees blushed.

'Oh, he wants us to buy . . . some of those things they always sell to foreigners.'

'Been here long?'

'Yes, fairly long.'

'I'm only staying a week. Then I'm going on to Italy. After that I'll go back home, to New Orleans. Ever been there?'

'No.'

People turned to look at them as they walked by; they were so typical of the foreigners one sees in the Paris streets, pushing their way ahead as if the place belonged to them, and talking at the top of their voices as if no one could possibly understand them.

'That's the street.' Kees pointed.

He was on his guard. On no account must he betray himself to this stranger, who might be a police spy or one of Louis's gang. Well, if he was, he'd get nothing for his pains.

The bar which they now entered was something quite new to Kees. He was impressed both by its appearance and its atmosphere. There was nothing French about it; it was a fragment of the United States dumped bodily on French soil. Round a vast mahogany bar, tall, strapping men of various ages were smoking and drinking, indulging in noisy backchat. The two barmen, one of whom was a Chinaman, were busy serving whisky and huge tankards of foaming beer; the big mirror behind them was scrawled over with inscriptions in coloured chalk.

'A highball for you, sir?'

'Thanks.'

Anyhow, it was a relief after the brasseries of the last few days. Kees was getting tired of always seeing the same objects: the nickel-plated globe mounted on a pedestal, which served as a receptacle for soiled dusters and napkins; the bulky volumes of the directory aligned in a small bookcase; white-aproned waiters, and a woman perched on a high stool at the cash-desk.

Here he could almost feel as if he had made an ocean voyage and landed in a new, exciting country. Listening to what was being said around him, he discovered that most of the men here were discussing the afternoon race-meeting, while a very fat man with a quadruple chin, in a loud check overcoat, was busy recording bets.

'You in business, too?' Kees's new friend inquired.

'Yes. Flour's my line.' He picked on that because de Costers handled flour and he knew something about it.

'I'm in the leather trade. Try one of these hot dogs. They're sure to be good here, like we have in the States, and what we don't know about sausages ain't worth knowing.'

People were entering and leaving all the time. A cloud of tobacco smoke hung round the bar; the walls were covered with photographs, many of them dedicated to the barman, of baseball and football champions.

Rather unexpectedly the stranger changed the subject and asked with an alcoholic leer:

'Say, is it a fact that French girls always fall for foreigners? I've heard you can have a good time in Montmartre, but I haven't had a chance of going there yet. To tell the truth, I'm a bit afraid.'

'Afraid of what?'

'Well, back home I was told there's a lot of sharks about, worse than our gangsters, and you got to keep a sharp watch on your pockets. Ever been robbed, you?'

'No, and I've often been in Montmartre.'

'Had any dealings with the women there?'

'Yes.'

'And they don't have a guy hiding in the bedroom?'

It took Kees's mind off the superintendent's knaveries, and he enjoyed feeling himself an old hand giving a beginner the benefit of his experience. The more he examined the man beside him, the more naïve he found him; even naïver than a Dutchman.

'Their friends aren't in the bedroom; they wait outside.'

'What for?'

'Oh, just to keep an eye on them. There's nothing to be afraid of.'

'Got a gun?'

'Good Lord, no!'

'When I was in New York on business I never went out without my automatic.'

'But this is Paris.'

The sausages were excellent. No sooner had Kees finished his whisky than the glass was filled again.

'Found a good hotel?'

'Yes, first-rate.'

'Well,' said the stranger, 'I'm at the Grand. It's fine there.'

He held out his cigar-case, and Kees took a cigar without compunction; after so many days' abstinence, and especially in such surroundings, there could be no danger in breaking his vow for once.

'I suppose you couldn't tell me where I can get an American paper? I want to see the market prices.'

'In any of the kiosks – there is one just up the street, not fifty yards from here.'

'Excuse me for a moment. I'll run out and get one. Order another couple of hot dogs, will you?'

The place was almost empty, as it was close on one; nearly everybody had left for lunch. After waiting five minutes, Kees was surprised that his new friend hadn't yet returned. Then he started thinking of other things, and, when he looked at the clock again, it was half past one.

He had failed to notice that the American barman was eyeing

him in a peculiar way, and that he turned to whisper something in the Chinaman's ear.

The whisky had set him up. He was now in fine fettle, quite capable of standing up to Lucas and the rest of them; and he decided to draw up forthwith a plan of campaign – something that would really stagger them and force the newspapers to sing a different tune . . .

But why did that fellow fail to return? Surely he hadn't lost his way? Kees went to the door, looked up the street, and saw the kiosk, but not a sign of the American.

He smiled grimly. So he'd been had; the man had decamped, leaving him to pay the bill! Another little disillusionment – but he was getting used to disillusionments.

'Another whisky, please.'

Why not get drunk? He felt sure of keeping his head, well enough anyhow not to betray himself whatever happened, and to do – what he meant to do.

To pass the time, he started putting francs into a slot-machine which dispensed slabs of chewing gum, then asked for another cigar, as he had dropped his when going out into the street. As he was lighting it, he discovered that the room was completely empty but for the Chinaman, who was having his lunch in a corner, and the other barman, who was tidying up the bar.

Very smart that fellow thought himself, no doubt, playing the guileless tourist and leaving Kees to pay for a few whiskies-and-sodas and a brace or two of sausages! True, Kees was far from rich, and he desperately needed what little money he possessed; it was almost a matter of life or death for him. For he had expenses which an ordinary man escapes; for instance, that of buying a new shirt every few days, as he couldn't send his linen to a laundry.

Why not have another sausage? That would save a lunch.

Another idea occurred to him; he might spend the afternoon at the races, for it was depressing roaming the streets of Paris all the time.

He was just opening his mouth when the barman, too, started to speak, and Kees let him have the first word.

'Excuse my asking you, but do you know the gentleman who was with you just now?'

What should he answer: Yes or No?

'Well – er – I know him slightly.'

The barman went on in a rather embarrassed tone:

'And do you know what he does for a living?'

'Yes, he's in the leather trade.'

The Chinaman in the corner was craning his neck, listening, and Kees guessed that something unpleasant was impending. For a moment he felt inclined to take to his heels then and there.

'Then he's had you!'

'What do you mean?'

'I didn't dare to put you wise – for one thing, because there were so many folks about, and of course I couldn't be sure you weren't a friend of his.' And, moving a bottle of gin on to another shelf, the barman sighed: 'So I expect it means I'll have to hold the baby!'

'What are you getting at?'

'You'll find out soon enough. Had you much money on you?'

'A fair amount.'

'Try to find your wallet. I don't know what pocket you keep it in, but I'll lay you a dollar to a cent it isn't there.'

Kees patted his pockets and felt his throat tighten. Sure enough, the wallet was gone.

'Didn't you notice that every time he made a wisecrack he dug you in the ribs? Oh, he's up to all the tricks. I've known him for years. He's one of the smartest pickpockets in Europe.'

For a moment Kees closed his eyes. Meanwhile his hand was groping for something in his overcoat pocket.

As if the theft of all his money, the only means he had of keeping up the struggle, were not enough, the American – but perhaps that, too, was a lie, and the man was no more American than he! – had taken his razor as well. Probably the shape of the box, like that of the boxes used by jewellers, had misled him.

Thousands of people in Paris might have had their pockets picked that day, and for most of them it would have meant only the loss of a larger or a smaller sum. But there was one man in Paris, one man only, for whom twelve hundred francs and a razor were all that stood between him and utter ruin. And that man was himself! What a foul trick for chance to play on him!

As a matter of fact he'd had a sort of premonition early in the morning, when he was reading the newspaper, that his luck was turning – for the worse. Then he'd fancied a lull had come and things were looking better. He had welcomed his new friend's babble, the whisky, and the sausages – a respite from his endless self-communings.

'Yes, I'm sorry I didn't warn you. But, for one thing, you never looked my way. And then, as I've just told you, for all I knew you were a friend of his, perhaps one of his gang.'

Kees smiled politely while the man made his excuses.

'I hope you hadn't a lot of money on you.'

'Oh no, very little really.' Kees's smile remained angelic. For what he'd lost was neither a lot nor a little; he had lost all. The most a man can lose – idiotically, by sheer bad luck. Yes, decidedly, like Louis and the rest of them, chance was hitting below the belt.

Somehow he couldn't tear himself away from the bar, though he averted his eyes, for he had a feeling that tears were welling up in them. And why not? Could anything have been more damnably unjust than what had just befallen him?

'Do you live far from here?' the barman asked.

'Yes, quite a long way.'

'Listen! You're an honest-looking guy and I'll lend you twenty francs for your taxi. You might do worse than report that fellow to the police; it's about time he had a spell in clink.'

Kees nodded. He'd have liked to sit down and think things out, bury his face in his hands and give way to tears – or why not laughter? What had happened was more than stupid; it was disgusting! Really, he hadn't deserved such rotten luck.

For, after all, what had he done? Well, there was one small thing, of course but he thought that was justifiable. He had acted unthinkingly, out of dislike for that girl Rose. Not that he had anything definite against her; it was a case of hatred at first sight. So he'd given information to the superintendent against the gang . . .

But surely this outrageous blow that fate had dealt him was out of all proportion . . . ?

He took the twenty francs that the barman handed him, then looking up, saw his face in the glass, criss-crossed by scrawls in coloured chalk; a face expressing nothing, neither anguish nor despair, hope nor fear. Its blankness reminded him of a face he had seen ten years before in Groningen, that of a man who had just been run over by a tram and had both legs cut off. But the injured man didn't know that yet; the pain had not had time to make itself felt. And, sprawling in the road, he gazed up, completely puzzled by the women who fainted as they caught sight of him, and wondered what on earth was wrong with them and with himself, and why he was lying there surrounded by an excited crowd.

'Please excuse me,' Kees murmured. 'And thank you.'

He went to the door and started walking blindly ahead, unconscious of the people who brushed against him, and of the fact that he was talking to himself aloud.

From the chaos of his mind one thought stood out in sharp relief. They were playing a foul game, because they knew that

that was the only way in which they could catch him, for they realized he was cleverer than they, and fair means wouldn't work.

Superintendent Lucas, who refused to let his portrait appear, was a glaring instance. He resorted to the tricks of a card-sharp, pretending to be in Lyons and to know nothing about the arrest of the Juvisy gang. Louis, too, was cheating, playing up to the police. And so was Jeanne.

Kees would never have believed it of her. If the conduct of the others roused his anger and disgust, hers cut him to the quick, for he had always assumed there was a tacit understanding between them. The fact he hadn't killed her proved it.

And now chance, too, was double-crossing him. It had thrown across his path that awful American who could do nothing better than pick his neighbours' pockets. And who certainly would have no use for a sixteen-franc razor . . .

It was all too idiotic for words; it was terrible!

I I

*How Kees Popinga learnt that a tramp's outfit
costs seventy francs, and how he preferred to
go naked*

Thinking was, perhaps, even more exhausting than walking
the streets. Especially as Kees had resolved to make a thorough
job of it this time; to review his position under all its aspects
and leave nothing out.

Only – a tiresome fellow called Lucas and a nonentity called
Louis had decided he was no longer to be able to think in
peace, and a jovial pickpocket had completed the good work
by making it impossible for him even to sit down.

For to sit down in Paris costs money, during the winter
months anyhow. At five in the afternoon Kees had been
reduced to entering a church where rows and rows of candles
guttered before the shrine of a saint he'd never heard of. After
that he had lost track of where he went. Not that it mattered.
What mattered was that, just as he was getting his thoughts
into some sort of order, someone stared at him – which gave
him such a turn that they all flew out of his head, and he found
it almost impossible to get his mind to march again.

Another trouble was that now and again some silly little
thought would float up into his mind, and, developing an
absurd importance, switch his attention off the crucial
problem.

How many hours he had been walking was nobody's business
and he felt all the less need for sympathy as he didn't feel really
sorry for himself. All he knew was that he had got to keep
moving, day and night; with only twenty francs in hand, hotels

were ruled out, and so were the cheap bars which remain open into the small hours, for these were just the places where a man is likeliest to get caught.

If he had been dressed in rags it would have been much simpler; he could have dossed under an arch of one of the Seine bridges as so many tramps do. But the sight of a well-dressed man sleeping in such a place would be sure to excite suspicion.

So the best thing was to keep on walking. No one suspects a man walking briskly down a street with an air of going somewhere. But he was going nowhere, and now and then, after making sure nobody was in sight, he halted in a doorway.

How far had he got with his deliberations? Just as he asked himself this a new thought waylaid him. It wasn't so much a thought as an impression. It had just struck him that all this recalled the night when Frida was born.

Why, he found it hard to say. There was nothing in his surroundings to remind him of it. He was walking along the Seine bank and had reached what seemed to be the out-skirts of Paris. Big factories loomed through the darkness, their windows a blaze of light, a red glow hovering above the chimneys.

Rain was still falling, and now it was coming slantwise. That might explain it; on the night when Frida was born the rain had been falling at much the same angle. And it had been about the same hour of the night. No, he'd got it wrong; it was during the summer that Frida was born and the sun rose earlier. Anyhow, that was a detail. It was before daybreak that Kees had gone out into the street and started pacing up and down in front of the house, bare-headed in the rain, his hands in his pockets, gazing up now and then at the bedroom windows. There were other windows lit up in the workers' quarter on the other side of the bridge, and he had imagined those badly brought-up people, busy washing themselves . . .

Vain memories, and he had no time to waste on them. It was

folly to give way to idle fancies and stand gaping at the river, which at this point seemed to divide at the entrance to a canal, when he had an all-important problem to decide, his fate hung in the balance.

He started walking again, and for some distance saw no signs of habitation on the river-bank. Then came a group of tall, gloomy houses in which the lamps were being turned on, and a small bar in which a man shivering with cold could be seen lighting a coffee percolator. Kees shrugged his shoulders. There was nothing to be done about it. Obviously he might creep in, hit the man on the head, and make off with the contents of the till.

But he didn't need to be Kees Popinga to do that. Such plans were not even worth considering. He had studied them one after the other all the afternoon, weighted every possible plan, and now his mind was like a slate wiped clean with a sponge.

For it was now too late. In fact, he'd always been too late; that was because his opening gambit had been wrong. True, he was more intelligent than Landru, than any of those others whose exploits had caught the public imagination; but all those others made their preparations, plotted everything out in advance – as he, too, could have done, had he applied his mind to it.

Still, it wasn't his fault if he'd made a false start. If that fool Pamela hadn't gone into shrieks of laughter . . . With this one exception he had made no blunder – of that he was assured – and one day they'd be bound to admit it.

Men were passing in twos and threes on their way to the big factory, and Kees had to keep a close watch on himself to avoid attracting attention; for now it was up to him to see he wasn't caught.

He had a task to perform. After that, things would move quickly. Meanwhile he must keep his end up, strain every nerve not to betray himself.

But it's no easy thing for a man who has been walking for ten hours in pouring rain not to attract attention.

The wisest course was to go straight ahead, to cross Ivry and then Alfortville. There was still some time before sunrise, and day was only just breaking when he reached a stretch of open country on the river-bank, studded here and there with bollards used for mooring barges.

The water was yellow; branches of trees and flotsam of all kinds were sweeping past in the fast current. A hundred yards ahead was a two-storey house, the lower floor of which was lit up. Kees could just make out in the grey light the inscription over the door: *À la Carpe Hilare*. At first he failed to understand; when he did he couldn't help smiling. Really, it was too absurd – to apply the term 'hilarious' to a fish like a carp, which has a particularly small, sulky-looking mouth!

There were arbours round the house – or rather iron trellises which in the summer, no doubt, were covered with verdure – and some pleasure-boats were moored along the bank.

Kees began by walking past the place with a casual air, so as to size it up. He saw a fairly big restaurant in which a motherly-looking woman was replenishing the stove, while a man, doubtless the proprietor, was having a meal on a table spread with oilcloth.

Satisfied by what he saw, he walked in, saying affably:

'Good morning. Vile weather, isn't it?'

The woman gave a start; he felt that for some reason she was frightened. Did she think he was going to attack her? And she watched him suspiciously as he sat down beside the stove and asked:

'Any chance of a cup of coffee?'

'I'll get you one.'

A cat was sleeping curled up on a chair.

'Good. And some bread and butter, please.'

He smiled to himself; these good folk had no idea who the

rain-drenched stranger was; no inkling that the next day . . .

He ate heartily, though he wasn't really hungry. Some minutes later, when the sun was up and the lights had been switched off, he asked for writing material.

They gave him some cheap, squared paper such as is sold in all French village shops and, after a long look through the window at the brown, swollen river, he started writing.

Sir, – In your yesterday's issue you published a statement to the effect that a police officer named Lucas (who for the last fortnight has been declaring that my arrest was a matter of hours) had released certain malefactors and ex-convicts and set them to track me down.

I trust you will publish this letter, as it will conclude an episode that reflects little credit on the authorities concerned, and spare them further trouble on my account.

This is the last letter I shall write you, and the last people will hear of me. For I have found a way of carrying out the plan I had in mind on leaving Groningen, when I decided to break with convention. By the time this reaches you I shall have ceased to be Kees Popinga and a fugitive from justice.

I shall bear an honourable name and have an assured position; I shall belong to that privileged class whose wealth and lack of scruple enable them to do exactly as they please.

You must forgive me if, for obvious reasons, I do not name the scene of my future activities – whether London, New York, or Paris. I may, however, say that it is in the world of big business that I shall operate, and that I shall have no more truck with women of the class of Pamela or Mlle Rozier, but shall choose my mistresses amongst the stars of filmland and the stage.

If it is to you, sir, rather than to another editor that I address myself, this is because a member of your staff, M. Saladin – against whom, I must admit, I had some causes of complaint at the outset – published a most helpful article yesterday in your columns.

Allow me to repeat (and I know what I am talking about) that by the time you get this letter I shall be quite inaccessible, and that M. Lucas may as well close the inquiry which he has conducted with such remarkable skill and tact.

And I shall have proved that a man, who so long as he observed the rules of the game remained a mere employee, can by dint of sheer intelligence, once he has cleared his mind of cant, rise to the highest position one could wish for.

Faithfully yours, Kees Popinga.

He nearly added 'paranoiac' after his name, as a last fling. Then, noticing the proprietor of the restaurant standing in the doorway watching the rain, he went up to him. As his eye fell on the row-boats moored beside the bank, Kees couldn't help observing:

'Are those yours? I've a boat too.'

'Really?' said the man politely.

'Only it's built quite differently. I don't think you have that kind in France.'

While Kees was describing the lines of his boat, the woman kept on fetching buckets of water from the river, preparatory to washing out the restaurant.

The queer thing was that, when speaking of the *Zeedeufel*, he suddenly felt his eyelids burning and had to turn away. A picture had risen before him of his little boat, trim and tidy as a Navy cutter, bobbing on the wavelets of the canal. Abruptly he asked:

'How much do I owe you? Oh, and by the way, how does one get from here to Paris?'

'You've a tram-stop five hundred yards from here.'

'And Juvisy?'

'You can go by train from Alfortville. Or else go to Paris and take a bus.'

It was hard to tear himself away. His gaze lingered on the table at which he had written the letter, on the cat sleeping on a rush-bottomed chair, on the woman who was getting down on her knees to wash the floor, and the man in a blue jersey like those worn by fishermen, puffing away at his pipe. '*La Carpe Hilare*,' he murmured to himself.

He'd have liked to make some remark giving them to understand that unwittingly they had witnessed an event of high importance, and to tell them to study the next day's paper.

The idea of leaving was distasteful. And he'd have enjoyed a glass of brandy, but he had to husband his twenty francs.

At last 'I'm off,' he said with a sigh.

Which was a relief to the man and woman, who had scented something queer about him.

His first idea had been rather different. He had intended to make his way to Juvisy on foot along the river bank. He had plenty of time before him, and could go by easy stages. But – another proof of his complete lucidity – it had struck him while writing the letter that, with the postmark of a place near Juvisy, it would give a clue to his whereabouts and defeat its purpose.

The wisest thing was to return to Paris. He took the tram, and the jolts made him feel sick, as happens when one is over-tired. Near the Louvre he bought a stamp and posted the letter, after holding it poised above the letter box for some moments.

Anyhow, he had no more thinking to do. All that remained was to carry out his plan, step by step, taking care to make no slips.

It was still raining. Paris looked its most dismal and there was something almost nightmarish in the sight of all those crowds of people in a frantic, futile hurry, and of the squalid streets round Les Halles where one stumbled over mounds of vegetable refuse from the market. For the first time he noticed the enormous number of shoe shops in this district, their windows crammed with footwear of all descriptions.

Perhaps he should have put in his letter that . . . No, the less there was in it, the better. In any case, it was too late. Too late for everything. He hadn't even the courage to take that drunkard's clothes.

For it wouldn't do to go on wearing this grey suit. And last night he'd had his chance. Near a railway bridge he had come on a drunk man lying on a bench. It would have been the easiest thing in the world to stun him with a blow on the head and then undress him. He would scarcely have noticed – a pool of vomit and an empty litre bottle of wine lay next to him.

Of one thing Kees felt sure: he hadn't refrained out of pity. It was something different, something that only he could understand. It was too late; that was the truth of it.

And, even if he'd grappled with it at the start, well, he knew now that wouldn't have made things much better. One of the papers had hit on the truth of the matter, though when reading it Kees hadn't realized this, and indeed had relegated the article to the pocket in which he put those which had no special interest. The article, which was signed 'Charles Belières', contained a phrase beginning: '*It is obvious that we are dealing with an amateur criminal . . .*'

M. Charles Belières had stumbled on the truth; Kees knew it now. The revelation had come when the barman told him his pocket had been picked. He was an amateur! That explained everything: why the superintendent disdained him, why the journalists wouldn't take him seriously, and Louis was hounding after him the others, the *professional* criminals.

An incorrigible amateur! For it was now too late to dream of changing his status, though of course he could have done so, had he set about it earlier and, above all, on different lines.

Anyhow, why tire himself with thinking now that all was over? Thought led nowhere; all it did was to give him a mental indigestion – like the physical one of which he was growing conscious. The great thing now was to procure a tramp's outfit, and nothing else mattered.

Some days previously he had discovered a small street, just behind the municipal pawn office, in which there were a number of secondhand clothes shops, and he started off in that direction. It was a quaint part of Paris, sordid but picturesque in its drab way. Looking up to see the name of the street, he found that he was in the Rue des Rosiers, and the name brought Jeanne to his mind. What would she make of it all? . . . How about pawning his watch? Hardly worth it; it had cost only eighty francs new, and they'd give him next to nothing.

He mustn't go soft, mustn't start looking longingly, like a child at a sweetshop window, at every bar. Alcohol wouldn't change anything. What mattered was his letter and, repeating to himself its phrases, he judged that on the whole it was a good piece of work, though he'd left some details out. What heading would they give it? And what comments would they make?

Another habit he must break himself of: this habit of stopping to look at himself every time he saw a mirror in a shop-window. It might attract attention, and was a silly trick anyhow. And it was making him feel sorry for himself – the last thing he wanted!

No, he must keep moving . . . Ah, there it was at last, that little shop he'd noticed one day last week.

He must remember, above all, to talk quite naturally and, if possible, to conjure up a smile.

'Excuse me, madame . . .'

At the back of the shop, amongst stacks of cast-off clothes, the form of an old woman could be dimly seen.

'I wonder if you could help me? I want a tramp's costume –

for a fancy-dress dance, you know. I'd make a good tramp, wouldn't I?'

Just then he caught sight of his face in a bamboo-framed mirror. It was deathly pale, perhaps with weariness.

'What's the price of an outfit like this?'

It was far shabbier, more threadbare, than the old suits which once a year, every Easter, Mum bestowed on an old beggar who called periodically at their house.

'I'll let it go at fifty francs. You can see it's got plenty of service in it yet, and the lining's new.'

It was one of the greatest shocks in his life. Never had he imagined an old suit could be worth so much, nor that a pair of shapeless, battered shoes cost twenty francs.

'Thanks. I'll think it over.'

No sooner was he in the street than he heard the woman's voice behind him.

'Listen! You shall have the lot for sixty, seeing as it's you, sir. And I'll throw in a cap as well.'

He shook her off with difficulty. Even if she came down to thirty francs, he hadn't got it! But he wasn't defeated yet; there were other ways out . . . An idea had just come to him, and his lips twisted in a sardonic grin; he knew what he would do, something that defied imagination. He'd stick at nothing, and follow up his plan to its logical conclusion.

'Yes, that should do the trick!' He caught himself up just in time. Talking aloud in the street wouldn't do; it would be absurd to give himself away at this stage of the proceedings!

He walked on. Again he entered a church, but a wedding was in progress and he preferred to go away at once.

'Can't you look where you're going, you damned fool?'

The damned fool was himself; he'd nearly been run over. But he didn't even turn his head.

Would it really have been ineffectual if he'd let himself be caught, refused legal assistance, and, rising slowly to his feet, confronted judge and jury. Then, after opening a file of documents, he'd have addressed the Court, calm and dignified, in a carefully controlled voice:

'You have all been labouring under a great illusion . . .'

Too late! It was unworthy of him, all this harking back to might-have-beens. By this evening his letter would have reached the editor of the newspaper, and the first thing he'd do would be to pass it on to Superintendent Lucas.

It was a curious sort of fatigue – more like a hangover; and mentally, too, he was in a curious state, at once befogged and lucid. For instance, he saw the people in the street as blurred, wraith-like forms, and now and again would blunder into someone, murmur apologies, and hurry on. Nevertheless, he had a very clear idea of what he was going to do, down to the last detail, found his way easily to the Porte d'Italie, and there inquired when buses left for Juvisy and what the fare was.

After buying a ticket he had eight francs left, wondered whether to eat or to drink, and finally did both. After he had eaten two croissants and gulped down some cheap brandy, there was no longer any possibility of drawing back, or of eating or drinking again.

But no one guessed it. The waiter served him like any other customer, and someone even asked him for a light.

And in the bus, which he took at about five in the afternoon, the people sitting round him noticed nothing.

A queer thought flashed through his head. Only a few days back, when he still had some money, he could, if he'd felt like it, have brought a bomb with him into a bus and blown it and everyone inside to smithereens! Or he could have derailed a train – quite an easy thing to do.

Still, if he now was here it was because he chose to be here, because he judged it too late to act otherwise, and, all things considered, the solution he had found was certainly the best.

How furious they all would be! As for Jeanne – well, it was

hard to say. He felt pretty sure she had fallen in love with him, though she didn't realize it. In the days that were coming she'd be still more in love and Louis would cut a very poor figure in her eyes.

He recognized the steep hill and the first houses of Juvisy, and got out of the bus. His legs seemed to be giving way beneath him, and it was some moments before he could manage to take a step.

One thing puzzled him. There were lights in the first-floor rooms over the *Goin et Buret* garage; did this mean that Goin, too, had been released? That was unlikely; the papers would have mentioned it. And, if Goin were there, the lights would be on in the garage itself.

No, it must be Rose; they'd let her out on bail. And this thought nearly spoilt everything, for it was all Kees could do to fight down an impulse to enter, give her a good fright, and perhaps . . .

Only, if he did this, his letter and all the rest of it came to nothing. For the same reason he mustn't enter the little café where he'd amused himself with the slot-machine and in which now, through the misted panes, he could see men in railway uniform lounging round the bar.

Perhaps he'd been unwise to have a meal. Still, he'd eaten hardly anything. Enough, however, to turn his stomach. He made his way along half-empty streets and round the station, by the level crossing. In the distance he could see the lighted window of the room that had been his, the window by which he had escaped.

If he didn't make haste his courage might fail him. The time made little difference once it was dark. The great thing was to find the Seine, and Kees soon realized that he had a false idea of the lie of the land, for though he walked a mile and more along the road parallel to the railway line there was no sign of the river.

He crossed stretches of waste land, allotment gardens, then some abandoned gravel-pits, where he all but fell into a water-logged ditch. Was it his exhaustion that made the road seem neverending? No, he could judge the distance he had travelled by the clusters of lights, villages, or isolated houses, dotting the suburban countryside.

Now and again, as a train sped past, he gave a start and looked away, muttering to himself:

'It's quite simple really, isn't it?'

Then he wiped his cheeks, telling himself they were wet with rain, though he knew better; some of the drops that reached his lips were salty.

Far up the road a moving speck of light appeared, and presently he saw a horse and cart approaching at a trot. As it passed he had a glimpse of a man and a woman huddled up side by side under a heavy rug, and he could have sworn he felt the warmth from their bodies fan his cheeks.

'Quite simple really!'

But it was a shame he hadn't had those sixty francs to buy a change of clothes! When at last the Seine came in sight, spanned by a railway bridge, he felt as if he had walked a dozen miles.

His watch had stopped again. It was a poor-quality watch, but what did that matter now? What was much more annoying was not knowing the exact meaning of that absurd word 'paranoiac'!

It was bitterly cold. Another meanness on the part of destiny. And there was no escaping it; he had to take off his shoes, which had the name of a Groningen boot shop inside them, and his socks, too, which his wife might have identified. He did this on the roadside under cover of some bushes. Then he took off his coat, waistcoat, and trousers, and shivered.

The only thing he could keep on was his shirt, for he had bought it in Paris; but he decided that would be silly, so he took it off too.

He felt the cold all the more as his feet were in a pool of water. The sooner it was done the better, as done it must be. He stumbled down to the river's edge and threw his clothes into the water.

Then he climbed the bank again. His lips were quivering. Just as he reached the railway line, beside a green light whose meaning he did not know, something extraordinary happened.

Till now he had been driven on by a sort of feverish energy; all of a sudden he became quite calm, and a peace that he had never known before descended on him. And at the same moment he looked around and wondered what on earth he was doing here, naked under a blue overcoat, trying to keep his balance on a slippery rail, so as not to hurt his feet on the ballast.

His hair and cheeks were streaming with water, and his teeth chattering. And he gazed with stupefaction at the river carrying away into the darkness an excellent grey suit, a suit made to the measure of himself, of Kees Popinga. Of Kees Popinga who had a house in the best part of Groningen, a stove of the best make, cigars on the mantelpiece, and a wireless set that had cost two hundred florins!

If it hadn't been so far away he might even have tried to go home, and crept in by the kitchen window. And next morning he'd have said to them, with a smile:

'It was quite simple really, don't you know?'

When one came to think of it, what had he done? He'd merely tried to . . . No! He mustn't start thinking again, especially about what might have been – now that the letter had been sent.

There was nothing for it; he'd burnt his boats. Already he'd let one train go by, on the further line; he mustn't miss the next. There was always the chance that a railway employee might find him, for he'd noticed railwaymen with lanterns patrolling the permanent way.

All the same, how silly it was! But that couldn't be helped. Silly as it was, he must go through with it, and he stretched himself across the right-hand track with his head resting on the rail.

The steel was cold as ice, and tears rolled from his eyes as he peered along the glimmering recession of the tracks into a black abyss, where presently a faint glow of light would kindle.

And then there would be no more Kees Popinga in the world of men. But no one would ever know that, for the wheels would have crushed his head out of recognition. Everyone would believe on the strength of his letter that . . .

He all but swung himself on to his feet; he had heard a distant rumble, and he was desperately cold. In a moment the train would be round the bend and . . .

He had meant to shut his eyes. But, when the train came in sight, he kept them wide open, bunched himself together, and held his breath though his mouth was gaping.

With a rattle and a roar the light bore down on him, and the roar swelled to such a din as he had never heard in his life before, so tremendous that he almost fancied he was dead already.

But presently there came a sound of voices, followed by an eerie silence. Only then he realized that the train had stopped, on the other line, and saw two men climbing down from the engine, and carriage windows being let down.

He struggled to his feet – how he managed it he had no idea. Nor did he realize that he was running, till he heard one of the men shout:

'Look! He's trying to do a bolt!'

It wasn't true. He was incapable of taking another step. He flung himself on the ground behind a bush, and then people came crowding round and someone flung himself on him, as one flings oneself on a dangerous animal, and pinioned his arms. A voice cried:

'Take care! There's a train coming on the down line.'

For him it was the end, and he didn't even notice the express roaring by, on the line that he had chosen. Nor did he pay heed when they hustled him into a second-class carriage, along with a man, a woman and the guard.

All that was their affair; personally he had lost interest.

12

*How it is not the same thing putting
a chessman in a teacup as dropping it
into a tankard*

All that was their affair. He had lost all interest in the proceedings, and it was with complete indifference that he let himself be marched, clad only in his overcoat, along the platform of the Gare de l'Est between two rows of spectators who craned their necks to have a glimpse of him and cracked jokes at his expense.

All this vulgar curiosity left him superbly cold, and barefooted as he was, he walked with dignity. At the railway police station, he was equally aloof, scorning to answer questions, and merely gazed at his questioners as at quaint, irrelevant objects. Why trouble his head about them, now he was absolutely convinced that nobody, nobody in the world, would ever understand?

All they gave him to sleep on was a narrow sofa, hard as a bare board. In the course of the night he was roused and made to put on a ticket-collector's uniform which was much too small for him – he couldn't even button the coat; but that, too, left him indifferent.

Just before dawn someone brought a pair of felt slippers with leather soles, as they had been unable to find shoes of his size.

It was they, not he, who seemed ill at ease, and they eyed him askance, with a sort of timid deference, as though he had some occult power, the Evil Eye perhaps!

'So you've decided not to tell us who you are?'

Kees merely shrugged his shoulders. Why should he help them out? Let them discover it for themselves.

Then he was bundled into a taxi which finally drew up in a courtyard of the Palais de Justice; he recognized the building. Thence he was taken to a fairly well-lighted cell with a bed in it. Some time later, after he had had another sleep, an excited little man with a small grey beard bustled in and started plying Kees with questions, pawing him all over as he did so.

Kees gave no answers. Still he had no idea yet who it was. He only knew when someone came bawling down the corridor:

'Professor Abram! Are you there, sir? You're wanted on the phone.'

So this was the psychiatrist who'd classified him as a 'paranoiac', whatever that might mean. The little man went out, closing the door carefully behind him.

What did Kees care whether he was in the Mental Ward of the jail hospital, or elsewhere? Sleep was the only thing he wanted, and provided they let him sleep, what did it matter where they kept him? He felt like sleeping for two or three days on end, on a wooden bench, on the floor, anywhere. Now that it was all over . . .

He had no watch, nothing whatever. They'd given him some hot milk to drink. Pending the professor's return he lay down again and went to sleep at once. How long he slept he had no idea, perhaps for quite a long time, for, when he was wakened, it wasn't Abram but some other fellow in plain clothes who, after handcuffing him, led him through a maze of corridors and stairs to an office reeking with pipe-smoke.

'Leave us now.'

From the window one could see the yellow waters of the Seine. An ordinary-looking, fattish, baldish man, seated at a desk, signed to Kees to sit down, and Kees politely complied.

The police officer murmured 'Hm!' once or twice as he scrutinized Kees, first from a distance, then from a yard or so away, and finally, laying a hand on Kees's shoulder, peered into his eyes. Abruptly he asked:

'What on earth came over you, Monsieur Popinga?'

But Kees kept silence. He wasn't interested, didn't even wonder if the man addressing him were the famous Superintendent Lucas. Nor was he interested when the door opened and a young woman in a grey squirrel coat stopped short on the threshold, and cried excitedly:

'Yes, it's him all right! But, goodness, how he's changed!'

After that Lucas recorded a deposition that Jeanne read over and signed, casting troubled glances at Kees from time to time.

So much for Jeanne! Whose turn next! Would he be exhibited to Louis, Goin, Rose, and everybody else, one at a time? It would be a boring business, but, now that all was over, what did he care?

If only they'd let him sleep! What difference could it make to them, since all these people could come and peer at him and paw him to their heart's content while he was sleeping?

For a time he was alone, then more people came, then he was alone again, then taken back to his cell, where at least he could lie down.

Did they imagine he'd be foolish enough, now, to let them know he wasn't really mad? Now that the last move had been made, and the game was over?

Really, they might have spared him all those futile journeys to the superintendent's office. Two or three times a day he was taken through those neverending corridors, up flights of stairs, and exhibited to people standing in shadow, who were asked:

'Is that the man?'

'No,' someone said. 'It isn't he. The man was smaller.'

They showed him his letters.

'Did you write these?'

But he only mumbled something that sounded like:

'Haven't an idea!'

Also they really might have got him a suit that fitted, and a pair of socks. For he still had no socks! And those people who, in a bleak, barn-like room on the top floor, had taken his fingerprints and photographed him, might have spared him the discomfort of waiting for a quarter of an hour, naked, in an ante-room.

Still, apart from these annoyances, conditions weren't too bad. Indeed, he was getting so used to them that he didn't turn a hair on the day of the demonstration.

Yet it came as a surprise; no notice had been given him. They took him to a small room where two or three unmistakable lunatics were waiting. Every quarter of an hour or so one of them was led out and didn't come back. Always one at a time.

Kees's turn came last. He was led on to a platform on which Professor Abram was gesticulating beside a blackboard. In a dimly lit hall some thirty persons were seated, taking notes; most were obviously students, but there were some older people too.

'Come forward, my good fellow. Don't be alarmed. I only want you to answer some quite simple questions.'

But Kees had made up his mind not to answer. He paid no heed to the questions, though he listened when the professor started gabbling away about him, using words even more technical than 'paranoiac', while his audience scribbled away for all they were worth. After that some of them came on to the stage for a close-up view of him; one man even produced a queer-looking instrument from his pocket and took measurements of his skull!

The silly fool! What did he expect to gain by that? It was *they*, if anybody, who were mentally deficient.

They had another bright idea; which was to lead him to a sort of sitting-room and suddenly, across a barred window, confront him with – of all people! – Mum, who had thought fit to dress entirely in black, like a widow, for the occasion.

'Kees!' she wailed, wringing her hands. 'Oh, Kees, don't you recognize me?'

No doubt because he gazed at her so calmly, she gave a scream and fainted.

What else could they think up? There must be plenty about him in the newspapers, but what did that matter to Kees, who no longer saw them?

Other people came to visit him; he could always spot them for what they were – mental specialists – as they invariably asked the same questions. But he had found a way of dealing with such visitors. He looked them straight in the eyes, with an air of wondering what they were making all this fuss about, and they very soon left him in peace.

For peace was what he wanted, and plenty of sleep. A meal now and then, followed by a glorious bout of sleep, during which he had rambling, but often quite agreeable, dreams.

One day they brought him a new suit. Mum must have had a hand in this, as it fitted him quite decently. Next day they put him in a prison van and drove him to a station. Then, accompanied by two plainclothes men, he was led to a train.

His companions seemed nervous, whereas Kees found the change quite to his taste. The blinds were down, but through the chinks along the side he could see people roaming the corridor, trying to snatch a glimpse of him.

'Think we'll be able to get back tonight?'

'I expect so. But it'll depend on the fellows who come to take delivery.'

Finally the two men settled down to playing cards. Now and again one of them gave him a cigarette and put it in his mouth for him – as if he were incapable of doing this for himself!

Probably everyone else knew from the papers what was being done about him; he alone was in the dark, but it was all the same to him. And he smiled when they were going through the Belgian, and after that the Dutch Customs, and he noticed that at a word from one of his companions the Customs officer refrained from visiting their carriage.

After the Dutch frontier a policeman in uniform joined them in the compartment, but, as he didn't speak French, settled down to reading a magazine.

After that events moved quickly; Press photographers were lying in wait on the platform and even in the corridors of the Law Courts at Amsterdam. Once again Kees was plied with questions, but he kept quite calm, merely answering with an amiable smile:

'Really, I don't know!'

There was a Dutch version of Professor Abram – a much younger man, however – who took a sample of his blood, X-rayed him, and sounded him all over. These proceedings took a good hour, during which the man never stopped talking to himself – which nearly made Kees burst out laughing several times.

Presumably that settled it. Kees was now the only one who didn't know his fate. Still, he felt safe in assuming they had certified him insane, as he had not been provided with a lawyer, nor was anything said about a trial.

And his next move was not to a prison cell, but to a big brick building on the outskirts of Amsterdam. From the barred window he could see a football field where matches were played every Thursday and Sunday.

The food was good and he was allowed to sleep almost as much as he wanted. When he was given physical exercises to do, he applied himself to them conscientiously.

He had a small, white, sparely furnished bedroom to himself, and his only serious grievance was that he had to eat everything with a spoon, as no knives and forks were provided. Still, that was a very small privation, and actually he was rather tickled by these precautions. So they all took him for a madman still!

Something there was, however, that was decidedly unpleasant: those screams that could be heard at night in other rooms, followed sometimes by heavy thuds. He, of course, never yelled; he wasn't so silly as that!

The doctor was a man of about his own age, and he, too, wore grey suits and gold-rimmed glasses. He was a plump, genial Dutchman, and called by once a day on his rounds.

'Well, old chap, what sort of night did you have? Still feeling bored? That's only a passing phase, you know. You've a splendid constitution and you'll soon get over feelings of that sort. Now let's take your pulse.'

Docilely Kees held out his wrist.

'Excellent! There's just a touch of, let's say, recalcitrance; but that will pass. You're not the first case of the kind I've handled.'

Then one day he was taken to the visitors' room, where, in the presence of a male nurse, Mrs Popinga had a talk with him. At Paris she'd collapsed before saying much, but she had evidently braced herself up for this second interview. She was in a dark, very plain dress, with a white collar; the dress she always wore to meetings of the Mothers' Union.

'You don't mind my talking to you, Kees? You can follow what I say?'

More out of pity for her than anything else, he nodded.

'I'm only allowed to come and see you on the first Tuesday of every month. First, I want you to say if there's anything you'd like me to bring you.'

He shook his head.

'I'm afraid you're very unhappy. But so are we all. I don't suppose you know how things are with us. I thought it best to come to Amsterdam to look for a job, and I'm working now at the Van Jonghe biscuit factory. The pay isn't much, but I'm glad to say they treat me with courtesy . . .'

He managed to repress a smile, though it had just struck him that Messrs Van Jonghe, too, distributed pictures to be stuck in albums – which must be a satisfaction to his wife.

'I've taken Frida from the school, and she didn't even cry over it. She's learning shorthand, and Van Jonghe will give her work as soon as she has her certificate. Why don't you say anything, Kees?'

'I think you've managed very well, Mum.'

The sound of his voice had an unexpected effect. She started sobbing, dabbing her red nose with her handkerchief.

'I'm not sure yet what to do about Karl. He's very keen on entering the naval training-school at Delfzijl. I wish I could manage for him to have a scholarship.'

So things were being fixed up quite satisfactorily, thanks to his wife, who was nothing if not competent. She came to see him on the first Tuesday of each month, and never spoke of the past. One day she announced:

'Karl's got his scholarship, through the good offices of your old friend, de Greef. He's been most kind to us.'

On another occasion she said:

'We've moved into new rooms. The others were too expensive. We're staying now with such a nice woman, an army officer's widow, and she's given us a very comfortable room.'

So everything was for the best. He slept a lot, did his daily dozen conscientiously, and strolled in the courtyard when the weather was fine. The doctor, whose name he didn't know, seemed to have taken a fancy to him.

'Is there anything you'd like me to get you?' the doctor asked one day.

For the moment he could think of nothing better than to ask for a pencil and an exercise-book. On the front page he wrote in big, carefully drawn capitals:

THE TRUTH
ABOUT THE KEES POPINGA CASE

He had plenty of things to say on that subject and it would be an easy matter filling the exercise-book; when it was full he'd ask for another. In fact, he would bequeath to posterity a complete, authentic description of his 'case'.

He could take his time about it, and on the first day merely drew some wavy lines, such as one sees on the title-pages of old-fashioned novels, beneath the title. Then he slipped the book under his mattress. Next day he gazed at it for a long time, but put it back again without writing anything.

As he had no calendar, the only way in which he could gauge the passage of time was by the first Tuesday of every month.

'What do you think about it, Kees? Frida's been offered a job as secretary to a journalist. But I wonder if it would be wise . . . ?'

Obviously! He, too, wondered. Still, why not?

'She'd better accept it.'

'Do you really think so?'

Wasn't it absurd, coming to ask for advice – at a lunatic asylum! But she got into the way of asking his advice about everything, even the most trivial details, such as in the past, in Groningen, gave rise to interminable discussions.

'Do you know, I sometimes think we ought to get a little flat with a kitchenette? The rent would be a bit more, but on the other hand . . .'

'On the other hand' – quite so! He nodded approvingly. Really, Mum was more 'mumsy' than ever, even though, instead of pasting pictures in an album, she now was pasting labels on Van Jonghe biscuit tins.

'They let me have their biscuits at half price.'

'That's grand!'

Since nobody could possibly have understood him, why worry? It was far wiser to make the best of things.

His conduct was so good that he was allowed to spend a few hours in the company of two other inmates, one of whom went mad only at nightfall, while the other was the mildest of men provided you didn't ruffle his temper in any way.

'Watch your step, Kees,' the doctor counselled. 'If you play any pranks, no more society for you!'

But why should he want to irritate those poor devils? He let them have their say. Then, when they had finished, it was his turn.

'Listen! When I was in Paris . . .' Then he pulled himself up. 'No, you can't understand. In any case, it's of no importance. But I do wish one of you played chess.'

He constructed a set of paper chessmen with leaves torn from the exercise-book and played chess by himself. Not that he was bored – he never felt bored – but out of a sort of sentimental attachment for the past.

As for the more recent past, he could view it now with entire detachment. He didn't even feel resentful towards Lucas. When a picture rose before him of the fat, bald superintendent prowling round him, patting his shoulder and putting questions that remained unanswered, he knew that it was he, Kees, who had won that match. What more could he want?

No, he had no intention of irritating his fellow inmates, or Mum, who hadn't changed a bit, or anyone else. He began to lose track of the passage of time, and had to smile when, one day, Mum announced, 'You know, Kees, I'm dreadfully worried. I don't know what to do about it. The Van Jonghes's nephew is in love with Frida and . . .'

How typical of the outside world, this agitation she displayed! It made him realize the gulf between her and a man of wide experience like himself. She treated this small domestic problem as if the fate of nations hung on it!

'What's he like?'

'Quite a nice young fellow really, and he's been very well brought up. But I'm afraid he must be delicate; he spent a good part of his childhood in Switzerland.'

It was too comical for words!

'Is Frida in love with him?'

'She says that, if she doesn't marry him, she'll never marry anybody.'

So that queer, sleepy-eyed daughter of his had developed a will of her own at last! Life could still be entertaining.

'In that case she'd better marry him.'

'The trouble is that the young man's parents . . .'

Didn't like the idea of their son marrying the daughter of a man who's in an asylum, no doubt.

Well, let them settle it between them, and make the best of it. That was what he was doing. In fact, he overdid it on one occasion.

One day the doctor, seeing him working out a chess problem on his exercise-book board, stayed for over a quarter of an hour, watching over Kees's shoulder, to see the solution. After which the doctor suggested amiably:

'Suppose we have a game now and then, at tea-time? I can see you're quite an expert.'

'It's quite simple really, isn't it?'

All the same, when he was facing the doctor over a real chessboard, and chessmen of white wood and ebony, he couldn't resist the temptation of taking a rise out of his opponent.

Only this wasn't the Groningen chess club, nor a Paris café, and on the table were only cups of tea. Nevertheless, noticing a bishop threatening him, Kees simply couldn't help whisking it away, while fingering another chessman to divert attention, and dropping it into his teacup, as formerly he'd dropped Copenghem's bishop into a tankard of beer.

For a moment the doctor could not imagine what had happened; then he caught sight of the chessman in the cup, and rose hastily to his feet.

'Afraid I must ask you to excuse me. I've just remembered an appointment.'

Naturally! He hadn't realized that Kees had done it deliberately. Yet why should he have denied himself the pleasure of recalling an incident of the old days?

'And *I* must ask you to excuse *me*,' Kees said politely. 'It's an old story, and would take too long explaining. And in any case you wouldn't understand.'

It couldn't be helped, and anyhow it was safer thus. Which was confirmed by the fact that next day the doctor requested Kees to produce the exercise-book in which he was supposed to be writing his memoirs. There was nothing but the title:

THE TRUTH
ABOUT THE KEES POPINGA CASE

The doctor looked up in surprise, evidently wondering why his patient had written no more. And Kees felt called on to explain, with a rather forced smile:

'Really, there isn't any truth, is there, doctor?'

READ MORE IN PENGUIN

In every corner of the world, on every subject under the sun, Penguin represents quality and variety – the very best in publishing today.

For complete information about books available from Penguin – including Puffins, Penguin Classics and Arkana – and how to order them, write to us at the appropriate address below. Please note that for copyright reasons the selection of books varies from country to country.

In the United Kingdom: Please write to *Dept. EP, Penguin Books Ltd, Bath Road, Harmondsworth, West Drayton, Middlesex UB7 0DA*

In the United States: Please write to *Consumer Services, Penguin Putnam Inc., 405 Murray Hill Parkway, East Rutherford, New Jersey 07073-2136.* VISA and MasterCard holders call 1-800-631-8571 to order Penguin titles

In Canada: Please write to *Penguin Books Canada Ltd, 10 Alcorn Avenue, Suite 300, Toronto, Ontario M4V 3B2*

In Australia: Please write to *Penguin Books Australia Ltd, 487 Maroondah Highway, Ringwood, Victoria 3134*

In New Zealand: Please write to *Penguin Books (NZ) Ltd, Private Bag 102902, North Shore Mail Centre, Auckland 10*

In India: Please write to *Penguin Books India Pvt Ltd, 11 Community Centre, Panchsheel Park, New Delhi 110017*

In the Netherlands: Please write to *Penguin Books Netherlands bv, Postbus 3507, NL-1001 AH Amsterdam*

In Germany: Please write to *Penguin Books Deutschland GmbH, Metzlerstrasse 26, 60594 Frankfurt am Main*

In Spain: Please write to *Penguin Books S. A., Bravo Murillo 19, 1°B, 28015 Madrid*

In Italy: Please write to *Penguin Italia s.r.l., Via Vittorio Emanuele 45la, 20094 Corsico, Milano*

In France: Please write to *Penguin France, 12, Rue Prosper Ferradou, 31700 Blagnac*

In Japan: Please write to *Penguin Books Japan Ltd, Iidabashi KM-Bldg, 2-23-9 Koraku, Bunkyo-Ku, Tokyo 112-0004*

In South Africa: Please write to *Penguin Books South Africa (Pty) Ltd, P.O. Box 751093, Gardenview, 2047 Johannesburg*

PENGUIN RED CLASSICS

ORLANDO
VIRGINIA WOOLF

'Exhilarating … lyrical, clever and funny' *Sunday Times*

Orlando has always been an outsider …

His longing for passion, adventure and fufilment takes him out of his own time. Chasing a dream through the centuries, he bounds from Elizabethan England and imperial Turkey to the modern world.

Will he find happiness with the exotic Russian Princess Sasha? Or is the dashing explorer Shelmerdine the ideal man? And what form will Orlando take on the journey – a nobleman, traveller, writer? Man or … woman?

'Wonderfully bold and inventive … pushes back the limits of fantasy' *Observer*

'Extraordinary' *Time Out*

For classic fiction, read Red

www.penguinclassics.com/reds

PENGUIN RED CLASSICS

THE SHELTERING SKY
PAUL BOWLES

'A novel touched with genius ... a story of almost unbearable tensions'
Evening Standard

Some journeys are best left unmade.

Kit and Port Moresby are Americans abroad. Struggling to save their marriage, they resolve to trade civilization for the wilderness of the Sahara. At first, the pair are seduced by the desert's beauty. But beneath the exquisite landscape lurk the dark undercurrents of an alien culture, and the relentless dangers of a hostile natural world.

And as they travel deeper, they might not only lose their way.

They could lose their lives...

'One of the most unusual, unconventional and gifted men of his time'
Sunday Times

'He let in the murder, the drugs, the incest ... the call of the orgy, the end of civilization' Norman Mailer

For classic fiction, read Red

www.penguinclassics.com/reds

PENGUIN RED CLASSICS

THE SORROWS OF YOUNG WERTHER
JOHANN WOLFGANG VON GOETHE

'Masterly and devastating' *Guardian*

You only find true love once.

When Werther dances with the beautiful Lotte, it seems as though he is in paradise. It is a joy, however, that can only ever be short-lived. Engaged to another man, she tolerates Werther's adoration and encourages his friendship. She can never return his love.

Broken-hearted, he leaves her home in the country, trying to escape his own desire. But when he receives a letter telling him that she is finally married, his passion soon turns to destructive obsession.

And as his life falls apart, Werther is haunted by one certainty:

He has lost his reason for living.

For classic fiction, read Red

www.penguinclassics.com/reds

PENGUIN RED CLASSICS

THINGS FALL APART
CHINUA ACHEBE

'The writer in whose company the prison walls fell down'
Nelson Mandela

'Gloriously gifted with the magic of an ebullient, generous, great
talent' Nadine Gordimer

Okonkwo is the greatest warrior alive. His fame has spread like a
bushfire in West Africa and he is one of the most powerful men of his
clan.

But he also has a fiery temper. Determined not to be like his father, he
refuses to show weakness to anyone – even if the only way he can
master his feelings is with his fists. When outsiders threaten the
traditions of his clan, Okonkwo takes violent action. Will the great
man's dangerous pride eventually destroy him?

'Unforgettable ... a work of great dignity and compassion' Jim Crace

For classic fiction, read Red

www.penguinclassics.com/reds

PENGUIN RED CLASSICS

WUTHERING HEIGHTS
EMILY BRONTË

'Passion and romance written like they ought to be' *Guardian*

In a house haunted by memories, the past is everywhere ...

As darkness falls, a man caught in a snowstorm is forced to shelter at the strange, grim house Wuthering Heights. It is a place he will never forget. There he will come to learn the story of Cathy: how she was forced to choose between her well-meaning husband and the dangerous man she had loved since she was young. How her choice led to betrayal and terrible revenge – and continues to torment those in the present. How love can transgress authority, convention, even death.

And how desire can kill.

'Unsurpassable ... I love it' Barbara Trapido

For classic fiction, read Red

www.penguinclassics.com/reds